I0631029

have love

Maddy Wells

Blue Heron Book Works, LLC

Allentown, Pennsylvania

Copyright © 2014 Maddy Wells

All rights reserved.

ISBN:978-0-9991460-5-7
ISBN-10-0-9991460-5-X
Cover design by Angie Zambrano

Blue Heron Book Works, LLC
Allentown, Pennsylvania
www.blueheronbookworks.com

Table of Contents

Chapter One

Everyone agreed that Alexandra Pavlo, my sister, was the most beautiful woman ever to come out of Samaria, Pennsylvania. You could demand a picture of this beauty, but listing specifics would diminish them, as, taken individually you could say, I've felt skin as smooth, or I've seen dancers move with more grace, or even I've seen fires burn brighter than her smile. And you might be right. But you can know particulars without ever knowing the truth. Truth is never in the details, which you can feed on endlessly like a vulture pecking on carrion. And who has the heart for that? Truth is what the heart sees in a shock of knowing, despite the scraps of evidence the mind presents trying to convince it otherwise.

Alex was my adopted sister and she had been with us since her mother dumped her in our garbage can in 1951, the same year I was born. My brother, John, who was seven at the time, was about to inter a dead frog in the can when he heard whining, thought it was our cat, but was equally interested to discover a naked little person lying on top of cucumber peelings and eggshells from the omelet my mother had made for dinner. The biggest scandal, as John told me and Alex when we were old enough to understand, wasn't her actual appearance in our garbage can, which fact astounded us anew every time we thought about it, but that Alex was found without a stitch of clothing. Her mother hadn't even put a diaper on her. The physician

who examined her said she wouldn't have survived the night in the
cold spring air. That she did survive was a miracle, he said.

What passed for a social service agency in Samaria was Mrs. Hughes,
a stern, stork-like woman whose veiled hat, sprinkled with black dots,
gave her the incongruous appearance of playing peek-a-boo when she
tried to catch your eye. Mrs. Hughes decreed that our mother was a
decent woman whose own brood was healthy and well-fed; that six
children would be no harder to raise than five; and finally—no doubt
to save Mrs. Hughes a good deal of work checking backgrounds and
cross-matching personalities, which was anyway a science with a
success rate no better than chance—Alex was ours. And so, like the
stars of other miraculous births, Alex became something of a god, to
me at least. And like all worshipers, I eventually came to believe that
this god was given to me, specifically to me, to transport me out of
my ordinary existence.

When we were children, Alex and I were inseparable. We were
nothing alike physically or intellectually, but we insisted we were
twins. We pointed to the fact that our eyes were remarkably similar;
the same sea-green almond shape curtained by black lashes on my
face, fairer lace on hers. That, though, was as far as any physical
similarity went. The chemicals that suffused her skin with light and
grew her limbs into exclamation points for the creation of the
universe itself, by some sad science turned merely functional in me.
My droopy arches supported a white and sweat-prone body, and
while my troubled skin technically kept things together, I knew, even
then, I was a lesser breed, fated to carry water to gods and goddesses.
Not drink with them.

When we played together, we didn't allow other girls in, mostly
because Alex and I didn't like other girls. As the sisters of four
brothers we knew what cool games were and, to us, girls seemed lost
in a hopeless, dreary world of dress-up and pretend. We derided their
games and were outraged when one girl, who had just moved into
our neighborhood, brought her harem of Barbies to a sleepover for

3

grooming and a late night dinner with Ken. "Doll babies?" Alex asked. We rifled through the hamper of clever doll clothes and mannequins in disgust.

We played with those Barbies in the only way we could think of which was to remove their clothes then stuff them in the garbage pail, tying the plastic bag around them tightly so they would suffocate. And they would have if Barbie's owner hadn't bawled until our mother rescued them. Rescued us. Our violence scared me.

Like other children, though, as soon as we could say the word, we became obsessed with sex. We knew that this powerful force, made more potent by its concealment, was the key to the universe and we hurried to learn how it was done. A boy at school, Jeff McGinley, had bragged that his parents were experts, citing as evidence his nine brothers and sisters, and he let us sit on a branch sloping across his front porch, which offered a clear view of the McGinley's bedroom so we could see for ourselves. Just as we were about to witness the crucial part of the act, a crow landed on our branch, its hellish cawing causing us to scream which alerted the McGinleys and possibly robbed Jeff of his tenth sibling, before we pulled each other down in our panic to escape, although not before we had good look at Mr. McGinley's breathtaking hard-on as he came to the window to see what the hell what going on. Alex and I suffered broken arms from our fall and I held my caste like a trophy, enjoying the constant pain, because it cemented the exclusivity of our relationship.

Even children, *especially* children I know now, understand power, and by the time we were teenagers Alex and I accepted the unspoken terms of our relationship. She would allow me to associate with her, and I would not reveal the fantastic truth I'd deduced: that while everyone including me adored her, she needed *our* adoration even more. When we turned our attention to boys, who were at first compellingly indifferent and later compulsively attentive, I could see that Alex was hungry for the adoration boys showed her. It was as if she didn't exist if somebody didn't love her. And, incredible as it sounds, she needed me even more than she needed the fickle attention of lovers. It's true. All stars shine brightly, but it's the ones whose praises are sung by poets that we notice. And I made sure that Alex was noticed. I echoed her life, made myth of her exploits, turned my adoring face in her direction so she could see her reflection in my loving mirror. Alex was the sun. But I was the moon.

Despite the glamour of her unusual beginnings and hypnotic presence, I didn't begrudge Alex her beauty. I wanted Alex to succeed, even if her high school idea of success—to be a rock star groupie—was, to me, a waste of time. For without her, how could I succeed? I was certain that I was destined to be the most celebrated actress of my generation, but I was realistic enough to have noticed that a pretty face opened doors, while my nose would be flattened in no time. I would have been a fool to let my best asset just wander off on a self-indulgent path while she could be doing something meaningful for me. I needed the entrée her beauty would give me. She needed my brains. And that was that.

My tenth grade English teacher, Miss Betts, counseled my mother that I was emotionally stunted and suggested sending me to the Barnes School for gifted children to complete high school and lessen Alex's influence. There I could develop my flair for drama. It was my only hope of developing my own personality Miss Betts predicted with the certainty of one who had seen this kind of thing before.

"Your daughter doesn't know who she is," Miss Betts said, peering into my eyes. "Here, look. Nobody's home."

My mother ignored the warning, upset that anyone would see anything sinister in her daughters' closeness. Her nurturing focused on corporeal, not emotional needs, and we were fit in that area. Her children smelled of cooked cabbage and Clorox, odors that signaled balance in her universe.

Other teachers, too, would try to separate us, to dim our power, and we would become despondent. Not eating. Not studying. Denying them the pleasure of our exuberant selves, until they relented and reunited the Yin and Yang. We were like Siamese twins, our souls funded by the same will. Together, we were formidable.

In the fall of our senior year, our father went to stay with a pretty young widow, Mrs. Pembrook, who lived two blocks away. When we saw him that Easter and graduation, he filmed us. He always had a movie camera in front of his face. It was a hobby of his, and although he had been doing that since I could remember, no one in our family except me seemed interested in the results. When I was alone, I would view the films compulsively on the projector that he had set up in the basement next to the washing machine. Alex and I were usually in the same frames, and though the camera adored her, it was my own faulty image that mesmerized me. I couldn't stop looking at myself, especially the selves I had discarded, at four, ten, twelve. I would perform in front of the mirror, redo scenes I had acted in real life, give them nuances that the originals lacked. I found that if I couldn't be beautiful, I could be fierce, kind, haughty, irresistible. Anything I wanted. I viewed myself as a work of art, never perfect, always in rehearsal.

I found I could make my face and body behave at odds with my real feelings. I could mime hatred or love and remain unchanged. It was like watching another person. The day I discovered how to do that, I felt an almost terrifying power. But I also knew that control over my physical being, while powerful, was not enough. To charm open the door of success, to re-write my fate, I needed beauty. I needed Alex.

So, was it love or calculation, this feeling that I had for Alex? I've lived with that question for years and have decided I should more accurately ask: can you love your jailer? Sure, I was imprisoned by the privilege and grace of being associated with such an exquisite creature. But only a cuckoo would fly a gilded cage.

The summer of 1969 we were eighteen. We knew that our future lay
outside Samaria, and in her first display of independence, Alex
jammed shampoo and make-up into one of the matching sky blue
Samsonite cosmetic cases we'd received as graduation presents and
boarded the bus for New York as an advance scout.
"Only one of us should go, it's easier to crash with folks if it's only
one," she said with more authority than I remembered giving her.

I saw her board the bus at Broad and Third and remained in
Samaria, sorting through our childish belongings to make room for
our new adult life. Everything had to go. Records, books, clothing,
diaries. I wanted no evidence of our former existence left behind.
Ruthlessly, I tore up photographs, postcards, lingering a while over
letters Alex had received from a boy several years older than us who
had gone to Vietnam. She had sent me to his welcome home party to
deliver the news that she no longer wanted to see him, but his
reply—his dark crew-cut head in his hands weeping until I could no
longer stand it and just left—I kept that to myself. I ripped his letters
into especially small pieces.

Then there was that box of junk I had shoplifted. Things we
didn't need: a 14-carat gold pen, dresses and bathing suits in styles
and colors neither of us could wear. I had stolen them as presents for
Alex, but she had only laughed at my daring in taking them at all. I
didn't just throw the pen away, I broke it, smashing its casing with a
rock, twisting the cartridge out of shape. I cut up the clothing, mixing
the pieces into unsolvable piles.

I destroyed other top-secret things that I'd never told Alex
about: the photos our neighbor Mr. Thwaite had taken of me when I
was sunbathing (he had given me copies under threat of exposure, as
it were); the condoms I'd found under the driver's seat of my father's
car; splotchy 8 millimeter footage of hoochie kootchie dancers my
father filmed when he was stationed in Corpus Christi that I stole
from his underwear drawer; and my father's warning, delivered as

part of a midnight confession to me right before he moved in with Mrs. Pembrook, not to trust men, because they only wanted one thing.

I bagged the refuse and dragged it to the garbage can. Several times during the day, I opened it to make sure that no one could use anything I'd put inside. Our things were imbued with our essence and I didn't want anyone else to claim it. I didn't donate our chattel to friends because we didn't have any, which was a lucky thing because I would have rid us of them as well. We would be starting with a clean slate.

John stopped by our empty bedroom and surveyed the place that had been transformed into a nun's cell. "Are you going on the lam?" he asked. He laughed, but his face betrayed concern. He was worried about Alex being alone in New York, saying he wished she'd waited for him, because he was moving there as well. He was a painter and New York was where the painter action was. I told him I thought that was probably a good idea. When I'd thought about him at all, and really there was no room in my world for thoughts of anyone other than me and Alex, I'd noticed that he seemed an extraordinarily lonely boy. I never heard him talking to girls on the phone like my other brothers, and he didn't go to his senior prom, although he told me not going was strictly a political statement. I thought New York, that world to which I ascribed as much magic and fluidity of form as Oz, would absorb him and give him what he needed, much as I believed it would do for Alex and me. And I was anxious to be free of his proprietary concern about Alex. As we would be in different arenas, I didn't tell him to look us up.

After two weeks Alex finally called. Everything was settled. She had prospects as a model, nothing immediate, but the woman at the agency had already sent her on three "go sees," proclaiming Alex's potential for a possible career if she stayed away from booze and drugs and men. And she had an apartment: a cool photographer's loft, which unfortunately, in my opinion, still housed the photographer. She talked so much about him, a man named Lance who had taken the photographs for her portfolio, that I finally asked her if she was in love with him.

"You'll love him, Nadia, you really will," she said, sidestepping the question. I could hear her struggle with a cigarette lighter. Finally a big exhale. She hadn't smoked in Samaria. "He's so into the moment. He never worries about anything." She laughed. "He thinks life just happens and you can't force it. I told him all about you." She laughed again. She sounded older, but I was too excited about the prospect of moving to New York to analyze it. It was the first indication, though, that her life was taking off without me.

"Is it hot there?" I asked, wanting to know what kind of clothes to bring, but also desperate to hear Alex talk about something besides Lance.

"Lance says this is the hottest summer he can remember in the city."

I could hear traffic, sirens, on the other end of the phone. "Are you in the apartment now? It's awfully noisy. I can hardly hear you."

"You don't have to be so critical. I've only been here two weeks and I think I'm doing pretty good."

"I'm not being critical. I just said it was noisy."

I hung up uneasily. It was our first ever quarrel. I blamed Lance's influence. This would change when I arrived.

I didn't bother buying new clothes for the move. Alex said that New York was such a separate world, anything I bought, no matter how with-it in Samaria, would be laughably out of style by the time I stepped off the bus. And I was not, no matter what, to look lost when I arrived at the bus station. "Pretend you know where you're going, even if you don't see me. Just find a seat and park it. Wear dark glasses so if you're scouting around you won't look like a mark."

"Aren't you going to be there? Waiting for me?"

"I just mean, in case something happens. It is THE CITY for God's sake."

I shared the bus ride to my new destiny with Madison Avenue advertising types and a few hippie parents, most of them no older than me. Some already had more than one child. I swore that would never be me, taking the bus with kids clinging to me like possum. This was going to be my last bus trip anywhere. From now on, people would drive me and be damned happy for the privilege.

A young girl in the seat across the aisle was juggling a crying brat with a Tarot deck, which she shuffled and spread on her lap over and over, apparently not liking the future she kept dealing herself. Scoop, shuffle, and lay them out again, a frown creasing her face. Finally, she turned and looked at me, her eyes large and unfocused, obviously stoned. She held out her infant.

"Would you mind?" she asked, cocking her head towards the restroom. "I haven't peed in hours."

I took the child and realized why she, and it must've been a girl because she wore a cheap pink crocheted jacket, wouldn't quiet down. She was soaked to her armpits. She hadn't been changed all day. I told her mother when she returned to change her kid's diaper, but she just shrugged, singing to her girl, re-spreading the Tarot cards on her lap.

While I felt sorry for my bus mates, I felt then, as I do now, that you will your own life. My bus mates' lives were runaway trucks with no brakes. They were as responsible for the miserable banality of their lives as I would be for the sparkling brilliance of mine. I felt smug and wondered, as we pulled into Port Authority, an underground, stylishly *noir*-like bus depot, if New York looked different if your baggage included other human beings for whom you were responsible. It was different for Alex and me. We weren't responsible for each other. We were just companions on the journey. I felt a rush of excitement that our lives were still to be written, not merely played out.

I pulled the sunglasses down from my forehead to cover my eyes before I looked around. Alex wasn't there. The advertising types stepped briskly away from the platform. The hippies conferred, lighting cigarettes and redistributing their loads, pointing in different directions, trying to figure their way and finally, drawn by the sound of tinkling bells and tambourines, they walked toward the escalator on which half a dozen undernourished looking boys in scruffy salmon pink robes, all with shaven heads, seemingly floated down to the lower level:

Hare Krishna Hare Krishna
Krishna Krishna Hare Hare
Hare Rama Hare Rama
Rama Rama Hare Hare

I was drawn to them too, and when one of the boys saw me staring at him, he singled me out for his chanting. My heart began to race illogically and I scurried to a bench spotted with blackened gum wads and sat down. Taking deep breaths to calm myself, I saw a man staring at me who'd been scanning the passengers as we disembarked. He was an older guy, more than thirty, short blond hair—too short to be cool—wearing a safari vest and filthy desert boots. He stood not more than two feet in front of me now and looked through my dark lenses. His gaze seemed to peel away my clothes as well as any grown-up pretensions I had wrapped around myself.

"We'll take the subway," he said, assuming correctly who I was. I wondered what Alex had said to describe me.

"Where's Alex?"

"At a go-see."

He wrenched my sky blue Samsonite cosmetics case from my hand—"It's not like I'm going to run away with your frilly panties," he said—and led me to the subway as if I were retarded. I was angry that, if left on my own, I would be hopelessly lost in the dank and humid maze of subway tracks and humanity, which seemed menacing and foreign. I accepted the tokens Lance bought me with a grunt, hating to be even that much in his debt.

The subway that Lance led me to was a zoo of multi-colored pelts, noises and smells. Lance talked a monologue the whole way to our stop. "You can live like a king in New York if you know the right people," he said. "You don't have to have a lot yourself, as long as your friends do."

"So, you don't have a lot?"

"I didn't say that. I meant you. You don't need much to live here 'til you get settled."

We emerged into the circus-like atmosphere of St. Marks Place. Music blared out of every open door and window. Street vendors hawked roasted peanuts and sausage from carts, the smells mingling with sweet incense that burned everywhere. The odors would have made me nauseous if I hadn't been so overcome with the excitement of actually being there. And the people! I felt like I was at a costume party: polka dots and wild Indian prints, cheap metal jewelry tinkling off wrists and ankles of both sexes. A group of tattooed bikers wearing leather vests over hairy tattooed chests revved the engines of their Harleys outside a corner bar. A tall man with blond braids sticking out of his Viking helmet brandished a shield, protecting himself from some energetic invisible menace. A man who looked like Salvador Dali was painting at an easel, pausing to look up at the fire escape above his head, but when we passed him and I turned to look at his painting, it was of a lake surrounded by pine trees. An old woman leaned on a second story windowsill and scowled down at the runaway traffic passing beneath her. Her disapproval made me inordinately happy. I stopped in front of a Magic Shop, the window displaying a hundred glasses of water, each with an expanding eyeball inside. Lance caught my gap-mouthed look and nudged me along laughing, dispelling my good mood.

We passed a man leaning over a car, his index finger on the hood seemingly holding him up. He looked paralyzed.

"Smack," Lance said.

His apartment was a loft in an old warehouse. He had to open three locks, which seemed sturdier than the structure itself.

"What do you have in here?" I asked. "Gold?"

"It's comfortable. It's cheap. I have enough room to work." He put my cosmetics case carefully on a futon shoved into a corner on the floor. The only privacy was a wicker screen barely longer than the mattress covered with an Indian print bedspread, bought for my benefit I assumed. Black and white blow-ups of women covered the walls. Stacks of books held up a door that was a coffee table and another stack held up the end of a sofa, a lime green velveteen monstrosity that had hosted decades of messy parties. A bare counter shone in the small kitchen. A beaded curtain partitioned off a waterbed with a giant hookah on the floor next to it.

"I work in there." He pointed to a door behind the master bedroom, a red light bulb on the wall next to it. "If you see that light on, don't come in. I don't care if the place is burning down. Got that?"

I nodded glumly. Under any other circumstances, I would have considered this a very cool place to live. Now I found fault with every detail. I smoothed the spread on my futon and sat down on it, crossing my ankles primly.

"That's it," he said, smiling. "Make yourself at home. I'll get us something to drink."

He fumbled around in the kitchen cabinet and finally came up with two glasses, blue with cut dots that came in boxes of detergent. We chatted and I tried to will away my hostile attitude, but I could not see Alex liking a man who would make her drink from such things. He was so old for one thing and he didn't seem ashamed of it. He was at least thirty-two. His dark blond hair was cut short in complete defiance of fashion and he wasn't wearing bell-bottoms. He moved with a confidence I found both unfounded and irritating. That confidence must've been what Alex liked about him. I was worried that she was limiting our possibilities. By tying ourselves to one man we would miss all the others. Although Lance was good enough company to share a bottle of wine with—he'd begun to make me laugh despite my foul mood—and was attractive in a way that I thought of my father's friends as being attractive when I wanted to test my feminine artillery, I didn't want to get trapped here. The city and our adventure had seemed limitless in possibilities and I was annoyed that such an ordinary person had already defined our parameters. I would have been happier if he had been incredibly handsome or incredibly rich. Incredibly anything.

He poured us some more wine from a jug on the floor as he appraised me critically.

"You don't look anything alike. For sisters. Maybe a little here." He pointed to his own eyes.

I accepted the wine and drank it quickly, wanting it to complete its numbing route through my veins. I pushed my glass towards him for a refill, but he didn't budge.

"If you're going to crash here, you'll have to learn to help yourself," he said. "I can't wait on you. I don't know what you've been used to, but I'm not your servant. Did you have servants or something in Philadelphia?"

"Philadelphia?"

She had lied to him. I ducked my head, cheering inwardly at this act of disloyalty to Lance.

"That teensy-weensy mansion on the Main Line. What does your daddy do, anyway? She's so damned mysterious. What is he, in the mob or something?"

He leaned against the sink, watching me. But I wouldn't help him. Alex was right to reinvent our origins. We were in a new city, starting a new life. We could be anyone from anywhere we wanted.

There was nothing so romantic about the truth that it was worth clinging to, and now that I was forced to think about it, I couldn't see our mundane beginnings giving us any cachet.

"Philadelphia is such a bore," I said.

He laughed nervously, and I was happy to see a man that old unsure of himself. "What's so boring about Philadelphia?" he asked.

"Are you from Philadelphia?" I asked, ready to be branded the liar that I was.

"No, but I'd like to know what makes two eighteen year old girls think that a big city is boring."

Lance pulled out a camera and held a light meter to my face. "I still can't believe you're sisters," he said.

"I'm not as pretty," I said.

"No," he said bluntly, studying the picture I made in his viewfinder. "But there's something else."

I put my foot surely on the path I was going to take and I could hear a huge gate clank shut behind me. I showed him the most flattering angle on my face and taking advantage of the years of practice in front of the mirror, my skill in making myself anything I wanted to be, I made myself sexy. "I'm more erotic," I said.

He put his camera down and looked at me. For the first time since I'd met him I smiled. He didn't. In fact, he looked a little shocked and put his camera away, while daring to look at me more boldly as we swam through the jug of wine.

We were pleasantly drunk by the time Alex returned. She seemed pleased to see the empty wine jug and sat next to me on my mattress, smoothing my wild hair from my eyes, and took a sip from my glass.

"You sounded so angry on the phone," she said. "I thought you didn't think I was a good scout." Her voice so effectively wrapped its cocoon around me that I was lulled into believing it was just us again. Lance was only a host to our adventure.

"What are we going to do with him?" I asked in a whisper, anxious now to know her plan.

She laughed. "With Lance? Here look." She opened her portfolio and showed me the pictures he had taken of her. I tried not to be enthused but the photos were breathtaking. He couldn't take credit for making her beautiful. But his photographs froze her at the precise second she was most herself. "If you don't like him, we'll leave right away. Right now."

"Honest?"

"I couldn't stay here if you were unhappy."

"I just don't know what you see in him," I said, although after only a few hours I had to admit I could see his appeal. "He's so ordinary. You'll be one of millions. Look at all these women." I gestured at all the black and white blown up women who pouted at us from the walls.

Lance had the good grace to go into his dark room when we started talking about him, so we were alone on my mattress.

"We'll go right now," she said. We hooked pinkies like we did when we were children, and I wanted to flee with her, wanted to pretend that our world hadn't already changed. "If you leave, I'll leave with you," she said, but by the tone in her voice I knew it would have made her unhappy.

We opened more wine and drank right from the bottle and talked of our dazzling future in New York. Slowly, I became assured that Lance really was just the man of the moment. How foolish I'd been to think otherwise. We talked of all the men who would love us and all the jobs we would conquer. We were too young to think our future might be already decided. How could it be? We hadn't designed it yet. How could we know that fate was feeding us our lines as if we were actors on a stage? That we had no control over what would happen that summer. The script was already written. Our only job was to play it out.

Chapter Two

In the two weeks since she had been away from me, Alex had acquired a new best friend, Blueberry.

"You can't be my best friend," she said, laughing at my fears. "You're my sister. Who has more significance, a friend or a sister?"

"Depends on the sister," I said, "and the friend." I tried not to sulk, but the people she gravitated to were such phonies.

Alex was meeting girls with all kinds of funny names: Blueberry, Yam M'am, Moon Child. The people who wandered through her life were losing themselves in pot and other drugs I wasn't yet familiar with, recreating reality for themselves within the walls of their own heads. They seemed to have grown disgusted with their animal selves and yearned to be plants or planets. It was like protective camouflage. If I'm a Blueberry, I can't be responsible for the havoc humans visit on the planet. I abstained because Alex and I had made a pact not to do drugs until we were established. Alex, I suspected, abstained in order to keep an edge of cool superiority.

In any event, Alex surrounded us with fruits and vegetables, claiming these people were more real for having doused their competitive and aggressive instincts. But in Blueberry's case, at least, I knew that she was planning to upstage Alex. I saw her looking through Alex's appointment book and making notes on a piece of paper which she jammed into her purse when I caught her.

I tried to warn Alex to watch her back, but she wouldn't listen. She loved Blueberry, "like a sister," she said.

"I thought she was a friend," I said.

"Friend, sister. Really, Nadia, what's the difference?"

Blueberry and Alex had become friends when they were assigned to a photo shoot in Lancaster, Pennsylvania, modeling clothes while perched on the backs of horse-drawn buggies. Amish people would be used as props. The idea of high fashion and Plain Folk mixing it up for a spread in *Seventeen* was so ridiculous I couldn't stop laughing.

"My God, those people don't even use zippers," I said. "They're going to be praying for your crass materialistic soul, Alex."

Alex and Blueberry didn't find it odd or funny.

"It's how they sell clothes, stupid," Blueberry said. She smoothed her shiny blond hair. "It's to get your attention."

"It's not dishonest or anything," Alex said, anxious for my approval. It was her first real job and she was so thrilled she almost forgot to tell me about it. She *said.* She'd remembered to mention it only as she was throwing underwear and toothbrush in a bag while Blueberry waited, chain-smoking Marlboros. So I told her that of course it was a legitimate way to make a living and I was happy. I was just going to miss her. That's why I'd said those mean things about it.

"Five days only," she said. "I'll be back before the weekend."

I wasn't disappointed that Alex would be gone for few days. I needed some time to reconnoiter, plan our next moves. It was hard to do with Alex wandering around, happy and busy. It made any suggestion to move on ludicrous.

More importantly, Lance left the next morning for a photo shoot in Mexico. He would be gone for a week. Once they were back, it would be impossible to be myself, so I made the most of the next few days, trying to chisel out a life amidst the clutter of theirs.

Noon the next day, I ventured out for the first time alone. Men with jackhammers and cement mixers did their best to repair potholes and cracks in the seams of the city, but I got the feeling that the place was deteriorating faster than they could pour the concrete. The constant pounding in the street was a backdrop of sound for the entire summer.

The neighborhood around Lance's apartment had the sleepless gaiety of a wake on its third day. Drugs were everywhere, lining the streets like lumps of gold in a hippie El Dorado and although Alex and I had our pact not to do drugs until we were on our feet, I made mental note of how sellers approached you and where they were.

Narrow single window storefronts housed boutiques garishly lit by strobe lights. The clothes they hawked were mostly Indian, some Mod mixed in for those who were straight enough, or cared enough, to iron their garb. Vendors with push carts sold silver jewelry and patchouli incense: the scent filled the air, defining the area as a tabernacle. I stopped for a moment, closed my eyes and breathed the exotic aroma. Even now, when I'm in a suburban mall and unexpectedly smell the stuff wafting from a head shop it brings me back to that day, that summer.

I stopped at a café and sipped coffee from a dirty cup, but I determinedly ignored it and scanned the want ads in a *Daily Mirror* someone had left on the table. The paper had nothing about auditions, so I looked for more mundane occupations. It was breathtaking how little I was qualified for. I had endured twelve years of education and was astounded to find that nothing learned in Samaria's public schools could be converted to cash. Even the most mindless occupations, like receptionist, required experience.

I put down the paper and stared into the mirrors that lined the walls around the booths, slowly becoming conscious of a man staring at my reflection. He wore an Army fatigue jacket with a name over the breast pocket I was sure wasn't his, because he had officer insignia on the collar and sergeant stripes sewn sloppily on the sleeves. I knew from my father's ranting about draft dodgers that a man who had actually been in the service could never tolerate violations to the uniform no matter what his politics. It would feel like a stone in his shoe.

Otherwise, he had the look of the boys we had necked with in high school. Skinny, long dirty-blond hair, impossible to resist smile, which I found no reason to resist. I turned to get a look at the real thing and smiled back.

Soon we were sharing a table and dismay over my career prospects. He dragged a long suitcase with him, which contained, he said with pride, an electric guitar.

He was only a few years older than me, and New York was not the first place he had ever been. Like me, he had been raised in an industrial town. Within five minutes we knew we had nothing more in common than that and our youth. But I found his world-weariness enormously appealing, because that's how I pictured myself in a few years. He was on the third stop of a goal to travel around the world. He had already been in Philadelphia and Washington DC and I liked that he wasn't impressed with them. I didn't imagine I would be either. I couldn't think of what would impress me, but I knew it wouldn't be contained in a lesser city than New York.

His name was Eric, but he was known "professionally" as Rick. He would play his guitar in a city until he had enough of the place and enough money to move on. He planned to circle the globe and land back in Indiana in five years. And after that he foresaw his future opening up again like a rose on its second bloom. All those possibilities thrilled me. Rick had been in New York three months and was crashing with friends until he got enough money to go to London.

"See these?" he asked, sticking his hands in my face. "Five years learning this thing." He pointed his head towards the guitar case.

I scrutinized his yellowed fingers, trying to make a connection to the guitar. It looked like he'd smoked a lot of cigarettes for a person his age, but that's all. I couldn't see what he wanted me to see. "Why? What's the matter?"

"The calluses, idiot." He sounded perturbed, then rethought his reaction and treated me to a phony smile. His teeth were as dingy as his fingertips. "You get these from jamming, from gigs."

He seemed pleased with himself, so I said, "Oh!" trying to appreciate his dedication to his art.

"You have to find out what you're good at and dedicate your life to it. You're not going to find anything in there." He pushed the newspaper aside. "What are you good at?"

I ignored the question of what I was good at, and he evaded the question that hung over the head of every twenty-year old male who wasn't wearing a real army uniform if he wasn't in school. We chatted about inconsequential things and made vague plans to get together later for a drink. Rick kissed me lightly on the cheek and said *"Ciao, bella"* as he left, which pleased me because I knew enough Italian to know he thought I was pretty, and I was still open to the possibility that I very well might be, if seen through the correct lenses and at the right angle. And if I had time to rearrange my face beforehand.

My job search stalled after filling out a few applications for receptionist positions. I needed that indefinable something to take phone messages and greet visitors. My charm wasn't enough. Or perhaps I had overestimated my appeal.

"Do you know who you'll be greeting?" one office manager asked me. "You'll be greeting dignitaries from all over the world. This is the United Nations!" I was clearly unqualified for that position because, for beginners, I needed at least a second language and a college education was essential. Just to say hello.

I got a copy of *Variety* and checked out the listing for auditions. There was an open call for *Oh, Calcutta!* "Femme standup—must be a dancer/actress who can sing, perform in the nude, when necessary. Bring photos and resumés to the Eden Theatre, 12th Street and Second Avenue, New York." I resolved to practice dancing that night in the nude, so I could try out. I didn't know anyone in New York anyway, so what difference did it make if I pranced around with no clothes on. And that summer everyone was talking about how beautiful the body was and how it was a sin to be ashamed of nakedness.

I made use of the time that Lance and Alex were gone by going through all of Lance's personal belongings. He had stacks of photos of models. They were undeniably beautiful and I wondered if Rick would still call me *bella* if could see these women. Or if he would, what superlative would he bestow on their flawless images? It seemed so unfair that I had to share a planet with these goddesses.

In the dark room, in a closet, were photos of these same women but naked. They weren't necessarily dirty, but they were certainly erotic and my heart beat fast as I flipped through, hoping that Alex hadn't consented to pose for him like that.

He had a small desk where paperwork was piled up. Unpaid electric bills, phone bills. Second billing notices to ad agencies for uncollected fees, typed on his old Adler manual typewriter, were stuffed in cheap white envelopes waiting to be mailed. "Dear Sir," one letter read, "If payment is not forthcoming, I will be compelled to alert my attorney." I felt a rush of tenderness for him. He was just small fry in a city of barracudas. But wasn't that exactly why I wanted me and Alex to flee? I wanted to be part of the eaters, not part of the feast.

I had just picked the lock on an old briefcase that contained more photographs of women—this time in probably illegal poses—when I heard the key and the bolt clunk out of position. I threw the photos in the case and shoved it back in the metal cabinet jammed with developing chemicals just as Lance came in the door.

"Oh, it's you," he said, relieved. He squinted, trying to adjust his eyes to the darkness. "You didn't lock the police lock. This isn't Philadelphia. The city is a dangerous place. You have to lock all the locks."

He didn't say anything about me being in his darkroom, so I just quietly closed the door behind and pretended I wasn't snooping. "I thought you weren't coming back till Thursday."

"The idiot models drank the water. They had mixed drinks with ice cubes in them. Those geniuses couldn't figure out that ice is water. Jesus. I would line up the shot then the model would bolt for the bathroom. A complete waste of time." He wandered over to his desk and absently shuffled his pile of unmailed invoices. "They'd better pay me, that's all I can say. Expenses, too." He looked around, suddenly missing something. "Where's Alex?" he asked.

"In Lancaster. Remember?"

He rummaged through one of his bags and pulled out a big package in brown wrapping paper and tied with coarse string. He cut the string and starting unraveling Margarita glasses and a pitcher. "She's going to love them. She says I live like an animal. Nothing matches." He admired the heavy blue glassware. "These are great."

"You got these for Alex?" My shoulder twitched, anticipating the load Lance was going to make us carry. We had to travel light to get where Alex and I were going. We couldn't be carrying glasses and pitchers. I couldn't imagine a scenario where we would do the serving. We would do our drinking at clubs where other people would pick up the tab. "I don't think she'll like them."

Lance seemed deflated by my assessment of his gift, re-arranging the glasses on the counter with less confidence than he had originally displayed them.

Nonetheless, he readied the apartment for Alex's return. Clothes disappeared into hampers. The beautiful wood plank floor, a relic of the shirt factory the building once was, was visible for the first time as Lance swept and swabbed. The model shots were taken down from the walls, and for the rest of the afternoon the red light was on outside the darkroom, as Lance created gigantic prints of Alex to replace them. Each improvement made me sadder and more anxious to leave.

I went to 12th Avenue, to the Eden Theatre at 2 o'clock, but didn't go in. I stood outside and stared up at the marquee, trying to make my feet move inside the building. An older man paused to look at me then the sign, *Oh, Calcutta!* He smiled as if he could divine my aspirations and found them ridiculous. I clutched my cloth bag to my stomach and hurried away. Even if my body passed inspection, my face with its horrible acne would never be allowed to grace the Eden Theatre. Maybe if I didn't have to take off my clothes, my face wouldn't seem so naked. It made no sense, but that's what I thought.

The day I'd arrived in the city, a man in a dirty white robe was sitting on the inside steps of Lance's building by the freight elevator. He had a brown beard and wore Ho Chi Minh sandals and had the general appearance of being old, but on second look, he wasn't more than twenty-five. One of his eyes was brown and the other a startling, almost artificial, blue. He had glared at me then, and I shuddered, but when I asked Lance about him later, he only said he was the Guru of Tompkins Square Park.

"He takes the bus in from Jersey City every day," Lance had said. "Or at least that what he says. I think he actually lives in our stairwell now. He spends most of his day in the park."

"For what?"

"What do you mean, for what?"

"What does he do in the park?"

"He's a Guru." Lance laughed, and I dropped the subject after he told me he was a harmless acidhead, trying to blunt his superior intelligence with drugs. The Guru had told Lance that his unhappiness was caused by being so much smarter than everybody else. He was lonely. He thought that if he killed some brain cells and became stupider he would find some companionship or at least accumulate some followers. At first this interested me, as I sometimes felt like that myself, but then Lance said, "He can do the *Sunday Times* crossword puzzle as fast as he can read the clues."

I was unimpressed with that kind of brains that I'd never thought of as intelligence at all, more like being a human encyclopedia. "As long as he doesn't hurt anyone."

"Only with his wit," Lance had said. "Don't provoke him."

Today, though, the Guru initiated a conversation with me. Maybe because I took the stairs instead of the elevator just to check him out.

"Out of the shadows and into the light, Pock Face," he pronounced, raising his hand in a Jesus gesture and blocking my way.

"Out of my way, Freak," I said, kicking him as I inched my way onto the steps. He grabbed my leg. I tried to wrest myself out of his grip, but he held on, forcing me to look at him. "You're just a fucking freak," I said, emboldened by the thought that Lance had said he was harmless. He wouldn't let go. I stopped struggling, but was off balance.

"Freak?" he laughed. He held on with one strong hand, while with his free hand he plucked out his blue eye and popped it in his mouth. He rolled it around, making smacking sounds before he retrieved it and stuck it back in the formless pink tissue that used to house a real eye. He laughed maniacally then released me to run up the stairs.

That night, Rick came by, unannounced. His gig was canceled and he wanted to see where I lived. He wore cowboy boots, which made him a few inches taller, and put his thumbs in his pockets as he stomped around inspecting the place. He admired Alex's pictures that crowded the walls. When I told him she was my sister, his eyes flickered with disbelief.

I hadn't told him anything about Lance, and he seemed surprised when Lance emerged from a marathon session in the darkroom and introduced himself. Rick was a musician, I didn't think he would be judgmental, so I was surprised when he grilled me later on our sleeping arrangements. He kissed me hard before he left. It was our first kiss, but I felt as if he had done it merely to reassure me of my worth. In my mind it wasn't a kiss at all, and he didn't call me *bella*.

The next day, Lance and I prepared a welcome home dinner for Alex, a roast beef and root vegetables, because, Lance said, they don't feed you on those shoots and he didn't want her becoming obsessed with the weight thing like most models. As it was, Alex was a little too thin in his opinion and he didn't want her to starve. We made the dinner together and while I hated the cozy domesticity of the arrangement, he made me laugh and I actually thought that maybe Alex could do worse than him. In a few years, that is, after we had already sucked all we could out of life.

Lance showed me a trick he had learned, to slit the roast beef and insert cloves of garlic. "The smell alone" he said, "is worth all the work." Although it wasn't any work at all. He was just showing off.

The roast was ready by six o'clock, when Alex was supposed to be home. He had made a pitcher of Margaritas, which we had drunk by seven thirty, so he made another. The roast was overdone by eight so we gnawed on that while drinking our second pitcher of drinks out of his proud Mexican glasses. We both were conscious of the place setting that hadn't been sat at. He brought out a joint, and nonchalantly fired it up.

"Want some?" he asked.

Despite the deal Alex and I had made not to do dope in New York until we were established, I grabbed it and took a hearty drag. Then another. We finished that and clumsily and funnily made another pitcher of drinks and by the time we finished that we stopped talking about Alex and he started kissing me, and I let him. Suddenly he jumped up.

"You know," he said, "With just the right light, you wouldn't be bad." He got a Nikon with a motor drive and began putting the light meter up against my face and sweater, then fired away. "Really, they're good," he said, and for a while I got caught up in the pleasure of having someone find me worth looking at. Though stoned, I thought about my uneven complexion and trusted his skill with lighting to even out the craters. I even hammed it up a little, as if I were in front of the mirror, becoming a thousand women, each with a different past and an even more interesting future. Pretending I had some tangles in my hair so I could play with it and flip it around a little.

"That's it!" he cried, "That's perfect. I always thought it was just your attitude that was keeping you from being beautiful." He put down the camera for minute and studied me. "You know, your eyes are just like Alex's. Same set, same color."

"We are sisters," I said. "Twins, remember?"

He let me into the darkroom, that *Sanctum Sanctorum*, while he developed the film and made contact sheets. We hadn't stopped drinking the entire time and when he finally showed me the contact sheets, I realized I was quite glamorous, and more full of my own power than I had ever been before. I even allowed myself an instant to believe that I was Alex's equal.

It was the era of free love and, while I disliked Lance on the principle that he would hem us in, define our world in tiny terms, I had nothing against him as a man who wanted to participate in the banquet I had envisioned for Alex and me. So when we awoke the next morning in the same bed after some hours of drunken, lurching love-making, I didn't feel guilty.

Lance, however, made a hasty retreat from the bed, not bothering with a good morning kiss. He headed straight for the bathroom to take a shower and I was a little humiliated to think he wanted to wash me off. I was sore, not because of Lance's prowess, but because of his birth-control method which was to shake up a Coke bottle and shove the foaming explosion up my vagina as a spermicide. He had read about this procedure in the *Joy of Sex*. Or maybe the *Playboy Advisor*, he couldn't remember.

"I'm not going to get pregnant," I'd told him, offended by his clumsy attempt to rid me of any part of him. Anyway, I was confident that since I had technically been a virgin until last night I was safe. I didn't think it possible to get pregnant the first time. The

Pill was generally unavailable to girls my age unless you lied and told the doctor you were engaged. Lance told me he got one girl pregnant and didn't want to go through that again, didn't want to go the back-alley abortion route again. "It's horrible," he said, "You don't know if you're going to see the chick again." *He* didn't want to go through it. His self-absorption was mind-blowing.

When he came out of the bathroom, with a towel wrapped around his middle, he seemed surprised that I was still there. I made a show of being in no hurry to scurry to my own quarters. He became irritated after he had made the coffee to see me still in his bed.

"Don't you have an interview or an audition or something this morning?" he asked.

I picked my toes for a while, trying to ignore the hangover that was building in my head. I did have an interview, receptionist for a magazine, but I probably wouldn't get the job anyway, so what was the point. Lance said it would build my character, just going on these interviews, but my character was the least interesting organ I owned at the moment.

I stayed in bed, thumbing through yesterday's newspaper. I wouldn't have minded if Alex had found us in bed, because it would have shown her that Lance wasn't to be believed if he said that he loved her alone. And part of me wanted to rebalance the equation between us. Still I was relieved when it was apparent that she hadn't yet made her way home.

"I guess Alex found a party," I said as Lance poured us coffee.

He grunted and put out some of the rolls from the uneaten dinner of the night before. In our haste to the bed we had left everything out. Even if it had tasted good, which it hadn't, the food would be spoiled. I started cleaning up the mess.

"Just get out of here," he said.

"I don't have to go to that interview," I said. "Maybe I'll never get a job. Maybe I'll just stay here."

"Just go! I'm shooting someone at eleven."

"It'll just take me a minute," I said, curious. Since I'd arrived, no models had come to his studio. I wanted to see what a shoot was like.

"Just get out. They get skittish if someone is gawking at them. They're like race horses."

I didn't have a large selection of clothes, two new pairs of bell-bottoms which nicely accented my ass—my best asset—so it didn't take long to choose something and be out of the door.

"G'bye," I said, but Lance was cleaning up and didn't seem to hear me.

I didn't want to use the stairs in case the Guru was still there, and somebody was coming up in the freight elevator, so I waited for it, telling myself I hoped it would be Alex. The gate opened, then the heavy door. A thin, nervous looking girl got out and looked around anxiously. She wore a midriff-baring top and tight bell-bottoms. She had the required straight long blond hair and carried her portfolio like a handbag. Her eyes narrowed when she saw me, sizing me up as possible competition.

"Lance Wilson, do you know which studio is his?" she asked, apparently hoping I wasn't one more obstacle on her path to success. If she was coming to Lance to take pictures for her portfolio, she was new to the business. That first night we had stayed up talking, Alex told me about the dirty tricks models played on one another to kill as much of the competition as possible. With a few exceptions, there wasn't a lot of variation among beautiful women. They were more or less interchangeable and aware that their marketability depended on more than just perfect looks. There was that elusive thing called luck. At her first go-see one of the girls told Alex that a friend, who looked "almost exactly" like Alex was turned away yesterday because she wasn't the type they were interested in. Alex believed her and left. The model who lied to her got the job.

The blond girl fidgeted with her portfolio. She looked as if she had one more rejection in her life she would go berserk. In my first act of kindness since I'd arrived in the city, I looked around and shrugged. "Lance Wilson? Got me," I said.

The would-be model gave me a condescending smile and I was sorry I had wasted any sympathy on her.

Alex came home the next day. Without Blueberry, but with a new girl named Moon Goddess, with whom she had hitchhiked from Pennsylvania. Moon Goddess was a giantess, 6 feet tall and at least 200 pounds. She had just come back from a trip to Kenya where she literally was a Goddess. She had walked into a village with her boyfriend wearing a halter-top that revealed the moon and stars tattoo on her shoulder. The natives, seeing this, fell to the ground at her feet, because their legends had it that their pale earth mother would come back to reclaim her children, and she would be carrying the moon and stars on her shoulders.

"It's so far out," Alex said. "In Kenya, she had a different man crawling into her hut every night to renew himself."

"The whole place wanted to renew itself through me. Jesus, was I exhausted," Moon Goddess said. She laughed and I could see her teeth were wore down unevenly, the teeth on the left side of her mouth almost completely stubs.

"She's a cooner," Alex said. "She softens the skins with her teeth. She's headed back home to Maine, but I'm trying to convince her to go to the agency with me. I think they would go mad for her."

But Moon Goddess left for Maine the next morning, to get back to her raccoons, and the three of us were left with ourselves. Alex didn't offer any apologies for her late show, and Lance didn't demand any explanations. She had a slightly disheveled quality new to her. Ordinarily she was remarkably put-together, especially for a girl who didn't give a damn about that sort of thing. The difference was that now she carried lots of bags, whereas before she had traveled light. She brought back souvenirs of the Amish country for everyone. An ashtray for Lance. I told her I didn't think the Amish smoked. For me, a music box with a twirling Amish couple on the top. I told her I didn't think that the Amish danced. It was against their religion.

"Is it?" she asked, irritated.

I put the music box on the tank in the bathroom, trying to make a joke of the present and in a few days it disappeared.

Alex was getting call-backs from go-sees. Lance was home quite a bit, photographing models and would-be's. He basically ignored me, so we didn't actually have to talk for me to know that he considered our indiscretion a one-time mistake that wouldn't be repeated, even if I had wanted it and I most definitely did not. I suspected that he hoped that not speaking about it would mean it never happened. The more silence that came between now and the event, the less real it would sound if I tried to bring it up.

I cooperated in his denial, but the air was uncomfortable, and with him and Alex encouraging me to find a job, to at least get out of the apartment, I started taking long walks out of our neighborhood and one day found myself on Orchard Street where it seemed every store sold leather or dry goods to the trade only, and in front of each store sat men in folding chairs wearing yarmulkes, white polyester shirts, and black slacks, reading Yiddish newspapers. One man looked up when I walked by and smiled at me.

"Come in, look around!" he said, getting up from his chair.

"I don't really need anything," I said, following him into the store, which was a button emporium. Shelves of small plastic bins, accessed by a rolling ladder, lined the walls from the floor to the top of the sixteen-foot tin ceiling. Rolls of ribbon were on giant spools in the front of the store. I wondered at his interest in me, when he asked, "Are you a designer?" and pointed at the dress I was wearing that Alex had brought home from a shoot. "My sister is," I lied and told him I was looking for a job, and I started work there that afternoon, minding the store and dusting the shelves for one dollar and thirty cents an hour with a ten per cent commission if I sold anything in quantities of one hundred.

It was a long walk to the button store from where Lance lived, but at least I had something to talk about in the evenings besides my usual complaints and it made me less likely to blurt out to Alex what had happened between Lance and me, but I had the feeling that she already knew and didn't want to talk to me about it. Or more precisely, that her own life was becoming so interesting, the puny events of mine seemed to her a little dull. She and Lance started making dinners together at night, and laughing about people I knew nothing about. People in the business. The way Adrian Colin, the photographer, tried putting the make on every model he caught in his view finder, "And he likes little boys!" they said together.

At first they explained their jokes to me, but it was forced and finally they stopped doing it altogether. I could feel their orbit tightening. Although they kept their lovemaking quiet, I knew what was happening just beyond my rattan screen and through the beaded curtain, and I hummed to distract myself, sometimes consoling myself that I had been in Alex's position that one night, and for once I knew exactly what it felt like to be her. Even so, it was the first time in my life I had felt lonely, because it was the first time Alex wasn't exclusively mine.

I saw Rick, of course. He had a regular Saturday night gig at a psychedelic basement rock club on St. Marks Place and a Sunday afternoon gig as a sessions musician at a recording studio in Brooklyn. I went to hear him play rock, none of it original and eventually my attention would wander, and I would be at the bar. I told everyone who asked, and everyone did ask, that I was a Gemini, although it wasn't true, I was a Cancer. But since we'd decided to be twins and share a birthday, Alex and I had made one up and decided that as twins we should be Gemini's. What else could we be? I read everything I could about Gemini's and tried to fit my personality to the profile. I looked at it as good preparation for acting. Once, I decided I should work out a persona for each sign. That would be really good practice. But I never got around to it.

I took up smoking, which I found titillated my nerves as well as giving me something to do. Rick tried to get me to quit almost the instant I started, saying that it was an expensive habit and we wouldn't be able to afford cigarettes on our budget once we started traveling together.

"And that would be when?" I asked, blowing tar and nicotine in his face. "When are we going to start traveling?"

He said a few times he wanted to meet my sister. He said she looked interesting in her photos that Lance had plastered around the loft. I knew why, of course, and although I wasn't in love with Rick, I liked him well enough and we were making half-assed plans to travel to London together when we had saved enough money. I didn't want to see the moon-struck look on his face when he met Alex and I didn't want to hear his amazement, as I had heard from so many boys in the past, that we really were sisters. Of course, if Alex were to come with us, he would have to meet her. I just wanted to choreograph the meeting and control the fall-out.

That night I tried to talk to Alex into moving on. I had a job now, dinky as it was. I had a good vibe from one of the auditions I had gone on. She was starting to make a ton on money modeling for catalogues. We could do better, I told her. We had so many plans when we decided to come to the city. There was no reason to get stuck in a holding pattern in the first apartment we crashed in.

"It would be premature to just jump without knowing where we're going to land," Alex said. "Let's just give this a go for a while. What else do you want?"

I wanted the life I hadn't yet lived. I wanted to be surprised at what the day would bring. I wanted to meet people I hadn't had the pleasure of meeting. I wanted to see their pleasure when they met me. I certainly didn't want to retire from a button store.

I forgot to mention the city. The Big Apple. The city that causes fear and excitement and that is not the same for any two people. Seven million of us crammed into a space so small that the city had to build towards to the sky to make enough room for everybody. They say that everyone experiences the city differently. It can be anything you want. Nasty panhandlers squat on corners where furry socialites pass on their way to lunch. Hippies float above it all, their perspective distorted by dope and head bubbles. Each sees the sidewalk from a different perspective. I expected to see the city from Alex's perspective. From the height of Olympus with all the privileges therefrom. I had grown accustomed to the ease with which beautiful women pass through life, not because, as I've said before, I was so beautiful, but because I considered the favor with which Alex was regarded as my birthright and I was loath to give it up. Maybe if Alex hadn't come to me so early I would have formed a character of my own and could have accepted her as my brothers did; as a nice but unessential addition to their lives. Even in games at school, when I look back on it now, I'm sure I would have never been chosen for teams if the others weren't scared of losing Alex's favor, her loyalty to me then was so fierce. So I blame her, too, for creating the half cripple that I'd become. I might have learned to walk if she hadn't been my crutch.

When we discovered boys, too, I liked to think that it was partly my charm that lured them into the net, but it wasn't true. Boys liked me well enough, and I was attractive in my own way; beautiful eyes and a great butt. But I knew they were using me to get to Alex. And when they met me first, as Rick had, they quickly forgot me when confronted with my dazzling sister. Who wouldn't? I had to content myself with table scraps but at least I was at the feast. I couldn't bear the thought of an eternity lived at the level of a button store.

Once, back in Samaria, Alex and I spent an entire week planning to become Rolling Stones groupies. She wanted Mick Jagger, which was fine with me, because I never found scurvy rock musicians as devastatingly attractive as she did. But I had to pick one, she said. You just can't go backstage after a Rolling Stones concert and not know which boy you wanted. I finally decided on Charlie Watts. I thought he was the most benign of the bunch and anyway he was married, and I figured he wouldn't want anything to do with me. We could just lie in bed and chat while Alex got it on with Mick. She had it all figured out, how we would by-pass security and obtain access to the Stones inner sanctum when all she had to do was show her lovely face.

We never implemented our plan, but the point is that this is as far as she dared to dream. A Rolling Stones groupie? I guess I didn't have the soul.

Chapter Three

The next morning I awoke to the now familiar sound of the garbage truck in the alley. I angled my watch to see its face reflected in the light from the street: five thirty. I lay with my eyes open until the sound of the empty cans bouncing on the sidewalk blended with the other sounds of a city whose energy ebbed and flowed, but never quite shut off. One of the things that Alex told me when I first arrived was that the city never slept. If you wanted a doughnut at 3 o'clock in the morning, someplace within walking distance would sell you one. It was a comfort to know that a fresh doughnut was there if needed. Later, of course, I would find out about the other, more interesting, services that were available in the middle of the night in New York, but then I was pleased about the food.

I had dreamt of Mr. Thwaite, our next-door neighbor in Samaria. When Alex and I turned thirteen and became intent on acquiring a tan, Mr. Thwaite took up photography, feigning artistic interest in the flora in my mother's garden in order to catch Alex in his viewfinder. The first time we caught him Alex wrapped herself in a towel and fled into the house. But I stayed outside and pretended to read, stretched, turned, squinted at the sun and removed my bathing suit top, tsking about tan lines, while Mr. Thwaite clicked away. We had a few such silent dates that summer and one the next. I got more adventuresome, coping poses I had discovered in my brothers' pornography. Mostly breast stuff. Arching back with my breasts tilted towards the lens. Massaging them with tanning oil. He gave me a print when I threatened to tell my folks. He died suddenly, not over that I'm sure, but how, I don't remember. Probably a heart attack, now that I think about it. People still died regularly of heart attacks in those days. I can't recall his face, only his silent adoration. I can't recall the dream, either, only that I had dreamt of him and woke up aching for more of that adoration. Wanting to see what he saw in me.

I became aware of the sound of dishes in our kitchenette and finally the smell of coffee. I got out of bed, not bothering to put something over the oversized Yankees tee shirt I used as a nightie, and wandered to the table where Lance sat poring over proof sheets. As usual, he didn't say anything in the way of greeting, so I helped myself to some coffee and sat at the table enjoying the scalding sensation on my tongue, which I believe did more to wake me up than the caffeine. I pulled one of the doughnuts from an open box that had been on the counter since yesterday morning and gently squeezed it until red jelly oozed out of the hole. I licked the confection and powdered sugar from my fingers and drank some more coffee, enjoying the struggle to wake up. I edged one of the photo proofs over to me to get a better look. It was the blond girl I'd met at the elevator. Lance had made her look a lot better in the photos than she did in real life.

"Don't get shit all over them," Lance said.

Chastised, I licked my fingers clean. "She's beautiful," I said.

"She's ordinary," Lance said. "But she has her moments. It's my job to capture those moments." He looked at me for the first time all morning. For the first time in days. "I can make anyone look beautiful. I even made you look respectable, remember?"

It was his first reference to our night together, and I wanted to protest that he found me more than respectable then, but I didn't. He stared at me hard, and I blushed under his scrutiny.

"If you stop eating that shit," he nodded at my doughnut, "and cleared up your skin, I could make you look beautiful, too."

I looked at the gooey pastry which was apparently my only obstacle to beauty and felt dizzy. "Not everyone thinks it's the most important thing in the world to be beautiful."

"I don't know a woman alive who doesn't think it's the most important thing in life."

"I don't," I lied, thinking of the auditions I wasn't going to. A little beauty would have given me a lot of confidence, even to do something that had nothing to do with my appearance. It would have given me a hell of a lot more confidence in life.

He laughed.

"Anyway," I said, angry that he had the nerve to criticize me, "you didn't mind my skin the other night."

Lance ignored my reference to our night of *ersatz* passion, and we were discussing the merits of beauty in our superficial age when Alex came in and sat down, eyes half-closed against the morning sunlight. Her lilac colored robe, a gift from the Spiegel people, flapped open carelessly. She had nothing on underneath. She smiled.

"I'm glad to see you two are finally getting along," she said.

"We get along," Lance said at almost the exact moment I was about to say it.

I saw in Lance's eyes a strange look, like he was in a conspiracy with me to make Alex happy. Please, his eyes pleaded, let her think that we get along. It would please her. It was a strange thought, that I would be in league with someone to protect my sister from unhappiness. Unhappiness that I, unbelievably, had caused.

"I told her that if cleared up her acne, I could do something with her," he said, his eyes never leaving mine.

"I always said you were pretty. You should be going to auditions." Alex rummaged through the cups on the shelf until she found the chipped one, oddly her favorite. "Get Lance to do some promo shots of you and just start going to auditions. Maybe then you wouldn't have to work in that dreary button store. No one can see your face from the audience." She swept her hand over her own face.

"It's not so dreary," I said, thinking of Shel Sonnenfeld, the owner, who believed that buttons held the world together. Buttons were responsible for every advance in civilization since the wheel, which incidentally inspired the button, the second greatest invention. You can't do much if your pants are falling down, Shel said. You can't be inventing cars and space ships and such if you think that at any moment you'll be exposed. Zippers, he said, would be obsolete in a few years, when people got tired of getting their skin stuck in them. No, buttons were the heroes of our civilization, silently working to keep things together. Not asking for anything except to be appreciated. But until they lose one, no one paid them the slightest bit of attention. He would lower his head as he said this, and I knew he had reduced his life to the level of a spherical object with two holes which existed for the sole purpose of holding up pants. Alex was right. Could anything be more dreary?

I escaped into the bathroom. I let the hot water run down my face and examined that face in the mirror imagining how it would look without craters. That's what I called them, craters. I thought if I uttered the most loathsome word, it would lose its power to hurt me. So, my acne scars were craters. But even with a smoother surface, my face didn't have the flair of even the lesser beauties who tromped through Lance's studio. I sucked in my cheeks and tried to mime myself beautiful. They were humoring me and I felt the humiliation of self-deception. I fled to my immediate destiny, the button store, late as usual.

To my surprise, Rick was waiting for me, sitting in the doorway. He had his guitar with him. His head drooped slowly, he was dozing off, then jerked back up.

I squatted down besides him. He looked troubled, as if he had been sleeping there all night. "Are you okay?" I asked.

"Nadia," he said, taking my hand, "I've been thinking."

"Not here, I hope," I said.

"No, no, I got in late from a gig. We jammed a little, and then I went for breakfast. And then I just walked and landed up here."

His hand held mine like a vise. He was a terrible liar. I shook him off.

"I think," he said, "that we should move in together." He sounded anxious, desperate, as if he were saving my life, when he was going to ask me to save his. His roommates had probably thrown him out, but instead of being a negative, I found it sort of romantic. No one I'd ever known had gotten thrown out of an apartment. It gave him an outlaw aura.

"What about London?" I asked. We always talked about London, a city of almost infinite possibilities we agreed. London was the source from where all life-worth-living flowed in those times. Every style nuance, every music breakthrough came from London. I also thought that it would be neat to acquire a British accent, which I felt would open up even more possibilities for me in the theater. "We could stay together in London."

"I think we should stay together here," he said. "You have no business staying with Lance and being one of his women."

I laughed, but imagined that perhaps men left their scent on you or an imprint that was visible only to other men. There was so much I wasn't sure of. "I am not one of Lance's women. What gave you such an idea? He's my sister's boyfriend. Come on, I have to open the store."

I unlocked the door, making the bell clank noisily, and turned on the lights. "Would you please turn on that contraption over there," I asked him, pointing to the coffee pot. It was a timed coffee maker, a fancy model from Germany, but the timer had broken years ago and instead of getting a new one, Shel insisted on manipulating this one. I had told him that they were cheaper now than when they'd first come out, but Shel wouldn't spring for a coffee pot that actually worked. I had to rig it so that it made any coffee at all.

"This place looks like it's in mourning," he said.

I had that reaction myself the first day I opened the shop. All the counters were covered with white sheets to keep the dust off. Buttons didn't exactly fly off the shelves and dust was a bigger problem than it would have been in a store with more popular inventory. Some of the more beautiful buttons, like the onyx with rhinestones, had been here for years, Shel said. I entertained myself by imagining the clothes some of these exotic buttons would hold together. I would have been heartbroken if someone had bought them.

I went through the store whipping off the dust covers. Rick watched, didn't help. "You're just an innocent, you know."

"I am not," I said, blushing because I thought of my bad behavior with Lance several nights ago. It was liberating to think that something as bad as a betrayal wouldn't even show. I'm ashamed to say that it presented the possibility that I could perhaps get away with even worse.

"You're like all these birds in New York who come from small towns. You don't have a clue which end is up and you act all sophisticated, but really, it's all new to you. And that's why you get into trouble."

"I'm not in trouble. Where did you get an idea like that?"

I folded the dustsheets with less energy than I'd whipped them off.

"You must make something here. Between that and my gigs, we could afford something."

"What are you talking about? What about London?"

"We can have London later."

The button shop seemed suddenly small. New York seemed smaller, too. All the centrifugal force I was counting on to propel me out further into the world, Rick's and Alex's momentum was slowing down. "What do you mean, later? I want to live now."

Rick laughed. "What's the hurry, you're only 18 years old."

"Yes, that's right. I'm eighteen years old. I'll never be eighteen again. I'll never have this chance again."

"What chance is that?"

I crushed the sheets and jammed them in the back room behind a chintz curtain. A person like me wouldn't get many chances in life. If the universe granted me any success at all, it would be because I managed to slip in behind Alex before they thought to check my credentials. Alex, who I felt was trying to shake me off, run the race without encumbrance. Time was critical.

Rick was my back-up, mostly because I thought he wanted the same things I did. Didn't he want to live, too? Did he all of a sudden want to settle down? The reason I liked him was his wanderlust. Without it, his body was a little too skinny. His hair too long and dirty. He trapped me between the wall and the red buttons, his breath heavy from a night of cigarettes and dope.

"You can't stay with Lance."

"What do you have against Lance?" I shoved him away and stood in the aisle. "The man's been nice enough to put up me and Alex for free until we can get on our feet. He buys the groceries and the booze. What else could you want from a guy?"

Rick put his guitar case on end and sat on it. "I don't know," he said. "It sounds stupid, but I don't have a good vibe from him. I think he's taking advantage of you somehow."

Usually Lance ignored me. And why shouldn't he? He had herds of models crowding in all day. He had Alex in his bed at night. What could he want from me? Witty conversation? I reddened. It wasn't pleasant to think that there was nothing I could offer a man as ordinary as Lance. What chance would I have with an extraordinary one?

It was only Rick's persistent stroking of the back of my neck that convinced me that Lance might be the littlest bit sinister. But it was still out of the question that I move in with Rick. I saw myself getting sucked down the swirling drainpipe to obscurity.

Shel came in and looked at Rick hopefully. A potential client.

"Good morning, sir," Shel said, ignoring me, the hired help, The Poor Little Button Girl. "Find what you're looking for?"

Rick gave a nod. "I'll have to come back later. I have to go to the bank."

Shel seemed surprised, but pleased with this news. Most of the buttons went for three cents a piece. It was unlikely that someone wouldn't have a couple of bucks on them, but still the specter of the young man coming back later would cheer him through the day until it became apparent that Rick wasn't going to come back and buy a bag of buttons from us. And then Shel would sink into a depression that would be solved only by his going back to his war room to plan another strategy. Shel had a marketing scheme. The old men with their *schmatte* factories who bought most of the buttons were dying off, as is God's will, he said, but there was nobody coming up to replace them. You need fresh soldiers, he said. When the front line goes down, the second row steps up smartly to take their place. That's the only way to win the button war. Where were the young designers buying their buttons? he asked. They couldn't all be using zippers, he almost spat out the word. Or, even worse, snaps. The thought that hip, young designers were using zippers because they didn't know he had the largest selection of buttons in New York sent him into a rage. "I'm right here! Right here with the buttons!" he would rail. I was a key pawn in his marketing strategy. As a young person with a sister in the business, I was to lure young designers in to buy buttons. As a young person, surely I had friends, other young people, to whom I could nonchalantly pass on the word about Shel Sonnenfeld's button emporium.

I haggled with a modishly dressed woman over the price of a few ivory buttons before lunch. She was a clothing designer with a storefront in the East Village. She was my only customer all morning. Ivory buttons are expensive, in large part because of the intricate and delicate carving on them and the amber glow they acquire with age. Anyway, we only had five left.

The woman, a peculiar New York type—that is, from somewhere west of the Mississippi hoping to be discovered in New York—carried a bag from Harrods department store in London. It was an ugly green affair, coated in a gunky plastic in defense against the British weather, hanging lightly, as if it were empty. It was empty. She gave me a sweet look as she fingered the five precious buttons.

"Five dollars is way out of line for a button," she said.

"They're genuine ivory," I said. "They're really works of art. Some poor craftsman whittled away at them."

She looked at me. "Poor *craftsman*? Poor me having to pay five dollars for one of these."

"We have others. Plastic that looks like ivory. You can't really tell the difference."

She looked suspiciously at the imitations I handed to her. "People can always tell the real item. You can't mix fake and genuine."

She tapped nervously on the counter, and I sighed as I returned the offending imitations to their bins. Before I could show her others that might be suitable, she was hurrying out the door. The bin that housed the ivory buttons was empty. They were in her Harrods's bag. The little bell jingled as the door slammed.

I had a few customers that afternoon, some teachers who wanted bric-a-brac for costumes for their pupils to watch the moon landing on television that night. Bric-a-brac and trim was how we made our money in the button emporium. The buttons, I am sad to say, were becoming curiosities. But everyone wanted bric-a-brac. Shel came out of his war room a few times to note the lack of young people, then went back behind the curtain, trying to devise a new strategy for attracting the second tier soldiers he needed to insure the survival of his enterprise. I went home that night feeling that I had let him down.

I wasn't too surprised when I saw Rick pacing in front of our building, his guitar and a small suitcase stashed in the doorway.

"Just be for a few nights. Until I can get my shit together," he said. "Those bastards didn't give me any time to get my shit together."

I invited him up, unsure really what to do with him, and we examined our meager finances. Not quite enough to get us to London and certainly not enough to get us our own place.

Although Rick had kissed me a few times, he had never pressured me to go further. I was curious about that. I had never known a boy to stop at a mere "no." But now he seemed anxious to cement our bond and ploughed away on me, over my protests that Lance or Alex could walk in at any moment.

He kept apologizing between moans of pleasure, and I knew by the apologizing that he didn't really care about me. But no matter. It was no better or worse than the other botched lovemaking I'd participated in. I had been right in my former resistance to sex, which I now had enough evidence to pronounce messy, violent, and inevitably ending with embarrassment.

As if on cue, Lance and Alex came in just at the wrong moment. They had been out shopping and had bags of groceries with long thin French loaves sticking out. They were talking loudly when they unlocked the door, but then hushed suddenly when they realized what was happening. Then they giggled and went behind their beaded curtain while Rick and I attempted to bond in the afterglow of his orgasm.

The dinner that night was wonderful. Lance made a roast, his only dish I discovered, and we got pleasantly drunk on cheap red wine. The only person who abstained was Alex who pleaded that she had a shoot the next day and needed to look at least human. Rick, naturally, was transfixed by Alex.

We ate cheese doodles from a bowl and watched the moon landing that night on television. It looked fake to me and I said so loudly and drunkenly. Who is holding the damned camera, I asked? It looked as if it were being filmed at a movie studio. Everyone laughed, but Lance asked how someone as supposedly brilliant as I claimed to be could be so damned ignorant.

"I trust my own eyes," I told him. "I don't believe all this damned pap the establishment feeds us. Maybe if you weren't so damned old, you'd be a little more cynical."

"Cynicism is an obnoxious trait, especially in someone your age," Lance said. He looked at Alex for affirmation, but she was suddenly distracted by something the news commentator was saying.

"It's impossible not to be cynical, the way you people fucked everything up," Rick said. "Nadia's right. This whole fucking thing is probably a hoax. It does look fake, now that you mention it. She's right."

He was talking about me, but looking at Alex, who turned to smile at him.

Lance jumped up suddenly. "Let's ask the Guru." He had a desperate edge in his voice. "He knows everything, right?" He went into the hall, hollered down the steps, but the Guru didn't answer and Lance came back to the sofa.

"He takes the five-thirty to Hackensack," I said, sarcastically, enjoying the fact that Lance could see Rick's and Alex's attraction as plainly, and painfully, as I did.

"Who's the Guru?" Rick asked.

Lance settled down and quietly lit a joint, which he shared with Rick. I sat on the floor in front of Alex and she absently stroked my hair, staring over my head at Rick, laughing at something stupid he said and I remembered the days of our groupie plans, unhappily. Her attraction to musicians. I'd been so preoccupied with fending off the full frontal attack by Lance on our duo that I didn't recognize the Trojan Horse I'd wheeled through the back door.

I had too much to drink and so I don't remember whether I asked if Rick could stay, but nobody said he couldn't, and after a few days when it was clear he wasn't going away, he was officially moved in.

Chapter Four

If Lance minded Rick staying with us, he didn't say. Before bed and sometimes in the morning I could hear their deep voices arguing over nuances of the Yankee's pitching staff. It was friendly talk, but I have since learned that men will talk of inconsequential things to anybody, especially someone with whom they have a blood feud.

Lance and Rick would laugh, but I never heard the joke that preceded it. What I did hear of their conversation ranged from the banal to the irrelevant. If they exchanged vital information, they said it out of my range.

Alex pretended not to notice the way Rick adored her, the way he dropped whatever he was doing when she came in the room, the way he asked her ten times a minute if he could get her something to drink or eat.

"You're kind of thin," he told her, getting out the ham which Lance bought and preparing a Dagwood sandwich which she would barely touch. He wanted a reason to keep her in his sights.

He tried not to be obvious, I'll give him that. He was cordial and asked her polite questions about the modeling business. Didn't she get tired holding those poses? Wasn't it tough fending off all the horny men on shoots? He basically made an ass out of himself, as if he had never been in the vicinity of a goddess before. He was a musician in New York, and New York was packed with beautiful women. But with Alex he was paralyzed.

Our sex became great, though. In the middle of it once, I had a vision, and granted I was stoned, we were always stoned, that I was an entire symphony orchestra and Rick was the conductor. The strings and brass were going all at once. Timpani banging. Brass wailing. He really put a lot of effort into it and I responded. *Response,* he said when we finished and lay back with our heads against the wall, did more to make a women attractive than the proportions of her body. He appreciated my *response.* And when we were alone behind our screen, he was vocal in his appreciation. He was full of theories and Lance and I found him increasingly a bore. We would roll our eyes at the same time when he started expounding, for example, on the bankruptcy of our parent's generation. Lance and I would catch the other's look, smile, but I would quickly look away, ashamed that everything Lance and I shared was poisoned with disloyalty. Alex, I noticed with no surprise, couldn't unglue her eyes from Rick.

She started spending more time at home in the evenings, just hanging out, and I allowed myself to believe that she was coming to her senses and was getting ready to take off with me. But she only wanted to talk about Rick. She never came right out and said it, she was cooler than that, but whenever there was an opening in the conversation where he could be inserted, there he was.

People, friends of Rick's I assumed, because he was the only one not surprised to see them, started coming over to get stoned with us. Folks would show up, bring out the dope and presto that was your evening. Lance had a hi-fi that he hadn't used in ages, the dust was so thick, and it was on top of the metal cabinet in the darkroom. He retrieved it and soon people started bringing records with their weed, pissing and moaning about the effect of a monaural system on their new stereo LPs. But they stayed. Someone found Lance's collection of records, too, and brought them out for derision as if they didn't belong to the host at all. The Tijuana Brass, A Million Strings, Xavier Cougat. Old fashioned shit like that. The album covers had half-naked women with lacquered hairdos, cavorting in champagne bubbles or whipped cream. Everyone mocked the music, as if the owner of such stuff had no soul, but I suspected Lance had bought the records more for the covers than the music inside. A case of being found guilty for the wrong crime. Anyway, when a Jewish guy with a curly Afro had too much to drink and decided to give the platters the fate they deserved, that is, he sailed them, one at a time, out the window Lance didn't protest. He laughed with everyone else, but removed the album covers to his locked darkroom.

The Guru began popping in as well, and we didn't throw him out. Why should we? We didn't throw any of the others out and no one even knew some of their names. Or even why they had come. Why not smoke your dope at your own house?

I did my first hit of psilocybin.

"Your first time, I'm so jealous," the Mermaid (so named because of a recurring vaginal infection) said. She poured me a bath with lavender oil, stealing flowers from a café flower box to strew about the water. "My first time, I was in the Louisiana bayou, and I lay down on the deck of my boyfriend's boat and looked up at the gnarly trees, and it was as if they wanted to screw me. Like I was having sex with this wet forest. Mushrooms are always sexual. The first time is always the best."

Her bracelets clanked against the edge of the tub as she checked the water's temperature. Her long Arthurian sleeves draped carelessly into the water, and soon she was in the water herself, fully clothed. Forgetting that it was my tub. The Mermaid had set my tab of psilocybin on a coaster on the back of the toilet, "like a sacrament, to be dropped at the appropriate time" she'd said, and I reached for it then, but it was gone, swimming, apparently, in the swamp waters of the Mermaid's very own bayou brain.

I soon found a replacement, although I didn't take it that night, because we never had a shortage of drugs. A physician, Dr. Lombardi, would show up wearing fatigue pants from which he would dispense pills, powders and capsules. "First do no harm!" he would shout to whoever hadn't heard him before, although everybody had. His brain played only one tape, and that was a newsreel of his experiences in Vietnam. "Why keep the fuckers alive to endure a miserable existence? Notice, I say 'endure,' because after 'Nam there is no life." We would patiently endure his ramblings which always ended with him saying "whatever the fuck" because then he would get down to dispensing his medicines, taking a tab or a snort for each one he handed out, as if treating himself for an incurable disease he'd contracted back in the jungle. Dr. Lombardi was a member of a bizarre class of politically disenchanted physicians who would give anyone a note saying he was unfit for military service. "Who the hell *is* fit for military service? For crawling around on your belly in the mud, killing the bejeezus out of other guys crawling around on *their* bellies in the mud," he would rail. "If you're fit for that kind of crap, you're a psycho! And the Army claims it doesn't want psychos! I got news for them, all it *gets* are psychos. If you're not one when you go in, you're certainly one when you come out!" The only person I ever saw him have what looked like a regular conversation with was the Guru.

Later, I learned that while Dr. Lombardi would write you a note saying you were too unbalanced to defend your country his endorsement meant nothing as his medical license had been revoked in Vietnam for dispensing excessive narcotics to amputees.

On rare evenings alone in our borrowed living room, Alex and I would drink wine and talk about our house guests and their shortcomings. Mocking others now seemed to be our only meeting ground, and if that was the game to keep Alex close, I played it with cruel intensity.

Rick was almost never around. He had day gigs as a session musician and on weekend nights he worked setting up sound equipment for the marquee acts that passed through the Filmore East. One evening when our living room was stuffed with people who looked familiar only in the sense that a group of young people from any era look the same, Alex asked me what I knew about him. How did I know he wasn't an ax murderer? How did I know he wasn't going to kill us all in our sleep one night?

"Those questions are so Samaria," I answered. The truth was that I didn't know anything about him and I was embarrassed to admit it. He was stumbling along the same road as we were, making up details to suit the moment, pretending he was in control of where he was at when in fact he was plummeting from one disaster to another.

"He would be kind of cute if he took a shower," she said.

"You know musicians," I said, not really knowing anything about them at all. Rick was the first musician who seemed even a little palatable to me. Alex was the one who wanted to be a groupie. I would have thought she liked his scruffy appearance. It didn't look as if the Rolling Stones ever bathed either, and she'd had plans to follow them around North America.

Reluctantly, I agreed to take her to the club where Rick now played three nights a week. Alex wanted to see if he was a *real* musician or if he was a charlatan. "I mean," she said before we left, taking time with her make-up and care with her clothes, "no one around here," meaning her, "has ever actually heard this guy play. Doesn't he ever practice?" She made it sound as if she wanted to protect me from this supposed ax murderer, who was by the way balling me twice sometimes three times a night and getting some excellent *response.* I knew she just wanted to see Rick making music with his magic guitar, his siren call, and I knew that as soon as that happened she would be lost. But I was powerless to stop her.

The club was in an old two-story red brick building with the name Hibernian Order of America chiseled in the mantle over the oak entryway. You would have never guessed it was a club in the daytime. It was only when lines began to form at dusk for the ten o'clock show and the mix master began his sound tests which you could hear through the boarded up windows that you would believe that the place had a secret life. At night, a bouncer named Leon, a former linebacker for the New Orleans Saints whose pension was a pair of damaged knees, sat outside on a barstool, letting in those of us who were deemed cool. I was cool, naturally, because I was a band chick. Otherwise I'm not sure I would have passed inspection. The other women there were breathtaking: long race horse types or lush earth mothers, like gypsies. Leon, needless to say, didn't even ask who Alex was. Her face was her admission.

The band was a loose conglomeration of keyboard, bass, Rick on lead guitar, and a temperamental male vocalist who looked like the sickly second coming of Twiggy. They were setting up when we came in and Rick smiled when he saw us. He put down his instrument and came over to make sure that we had a good table and something to drink. He kissed me on the cheek in a proprietary way and for a moment I wished that I loved him because it would be nice to love someone who kissed so gently. More than that, I wished he loved me. He shook Alex's hand and she seemed a little surprised at his gentlemanly manner. Or maybe she was surprised he hadn't tried to kiss her.

During the first set, an older black man with a Kangol beret on his head and a cigarillo between his lips, brought his rum and coke to our table, asked us what we were drinking. Or rather, he asked Alex what she was drinking. She answered for both of us and soon a bottle of red wine appeared on our table. His name was Thornton. Just one name he said, like "the Duke." We didn't know who the Duke was, so he said, "Cher?" and we nodded dumbly.

Rick came by. "How are ya all doing?" he asked, not really looking at us. He was scanning the audience and waving when he saw a familiar face. He obviously thought the set was a success, even though I had barely noticed it. "I'll be back in a minute," he said. A good-looking redheaded girl had smiled at him from across the room. "I have to say hello to a friend."

Alex's gaze followed him across the room to the redhead. She snorted. "Well, maybe he's not an ax murderer, but you've got a womanizer on your hands." She seemed unduly interested in the animated conversation Rick was having with the redhead.

"Can't he have friend?" I asked. "Doesn't Lance have friends? Lance has beautiful naked women in his studio all day. That's questionable form if you ask me."

Thornton expressed interest in these beautiful naked women.

"Lance is a fashion photographer," I told him. "Her boyfriend," I added to squelch any interest he might have in Alex.

A man in a modish outfit of polka dotted skin tight pants and Nehru jacket asked Alex to dance. He wore boots that had a three inch heel and was still shorter than Alex. They threw their bodies into the chaotic crowd on the dance floor, and I saw him shout something into her ear. She nodded and kept dancing, closing her eyes against everything but the music. A dreamy smile appeared on her face, which even the pulsing strobe light couldn't really distort. Although the dancers looked, on the whole, as if they were performing complicated maneuvers, when you analyzed it, each person did the same movements over and over again like robots. When the music stopped, the purple of the black light was still on and Alex's dance partner smiled at her, revealing a false tooth right in the front. Black lights went right through dentures, which is probably why they haven't endured.

"That's the owner," Thornton pointed at the man who was leading Alex off the dance floor, but holding her hand a little too long. She wiped it discreetly on her jeans. Finally he smiled and left to go backstage. Alex gave him a little wave, like a salute. "A good looking woman," Thorton said.

"We're sisters," I said, preparing for the onslaught.

"Yeah, you can see it," Thornton said. "Different daddys?"

"No!"

"Mothers then?" He grinned at Alex as she sat down, sweaty from her exertions in the claustrophobic air. "I have children with three different women."

"What are you talking about?" Alex smiled absently at us.

"Nothing. Here."

I poured her a glass of wine, which she raised in a toast, couldn't think of anything to say so took a drink instead.

During the second set, Alex seemed to enjoy herself and proclaimed Rick a good musician. She noted that the redhead, whom I had forgotten, had left. She seemed relieved.

"If I don't care, I don't see why you're making such a big deal about it," I said. "I'm not in love with him."

"You're not?" She looked at me closely and stroked my hair, moving the flyaway strands from my eyes. "I couldn't stand it if he hurt you. I couldn't stand it if anyone hurt you."

I blushed thinking that my love for her, the love I thought so pure, had been sullied so completely in a moment of lust with Lance. I wasn't worthy of her affection I told her, although I spared her the reason *why*.

"If you're not in love with him, I don't see what difference it makes then, I guess, who he talks to," she said.

We left without Rick, but his presence was between us. It was all she could talk about on the way home. It occurred to me in a sickening flash that Alex might actually be *in love* with him. It wasn't the loss of Rick that pierced me, because as I said, I wasn't in love with him at all. It was the thought of losing Alex yet again, before I had accomplished any of the things I wanted. I was hopeful, though, because at least I would be with them. And I rationalized that it would be more practical. Together, we could conquer anything because together we had it all. It wouldn't be so bad.

"He's just an average musician, Alex," I countered when she suggested that maybe I take another look at his attributes. "Anyway, he's kind of ugly, don't you think?"

She shrugged and dropped the subject.

"I can't go to the casting call with you tomorrow, I'm booked," she said apologetically. I had asked her to come with me to the open call for "Oh, Calcutta!"

I hoped that the director would so dazzled with her he would hire me when he realized we came as a team. "You don't need me, anyway. I can't act at all. You're the one with the talent." She gave me an indulgent smile.

"I can't show up without you. No one will even notice me!"

"You're giving me way too much credit," she said.

We walked a while without talking then she said, almost testily, "You're also putting a tremendous burden on me." Her shoulders shook slightly. "I feel like I can't be myself. An actress. What do I know about acting?"

I didn't say anything, but I felt as if she were a magic creature, changing into a bird to escape captivity. Slipping through my hands.

As I lay on my mattress waiting for sleep to come, she and Lance argued. They tried to keep their voices down, but the beaded curtain gave no privacy. The disagreement was whether or not Alex should have her freedom. She was bored she said. She was getting restless. It wasn't him, she said. It was just that she was too young to be tied down. Couldn't he understand?

They spoke for about an hour. The same words over and over, neither one hearing the other. The arguing stopped when Rick came home later. For once, he didn't sit on the edge of our bed nudging me to wake up so I could *respond*, but instead he stayed in the kitchen speaking softly to Alex. I couldn't make out the words but I knew they were together in a way that I had never been with him. I tried to feel rage or anger (after all I was technically being betrayed) but all I felt was immense pleasure that Alex and I were finally about to move on. A future with Rick, a nomad like us, held infinitely more possibilities than a future with a man tied to a darkroom and a closet full of paper dolls.

There was no relief from the stifling air in the loft and I thought their discussion would go on all night, so I decided to take a shower. I got undressed, wrapping myself in the towel that Rick and I shared and went into the bathroom. Lance had had the same idea. He was already in there, naked, standing in the stall without the water on. He was smoking a joint. He saw me through the wavy acrylic shower door and beckoned for me to join him. I dropped my towel, went in and took a huge drag on the joint. We finished the joint and started laughing, looking at each other through barely open eyes. We started stroking each other in a strictly friendly manner when one of us noticed Rick outside the door. I slid it open.

"Don't be a stranger," I laughed, pulling him in.

Lance had found another joint, from where I have no recollection because, as I said, he was nude, and we passed it to Rick first in a neighborly gesture. He took it, shed his clothes awkwardly, and stepped in. Alex was right behind, giggling, but refusing the dope. She still had her face to think about and a shoot the next morning.

We smoked the dope, and I said, "I'm trying out for *Hair*." I raised my arms and shimmied, feeling the ripple from my fingertips to my knees. When it got to my feet, I tottered and fell against Lance, who laughed and put me upright.

Rick grunted. "No you're not. Don't be stupid."

"They need femmes," I said, drawing out the last word. "Femmes who can do a nude *pas de deux*."

I turned to Alex. Her eyes were closed and she was smiling with the same self-absorbed look she had had on the dance floor that evening. Lance suddenly turned on the cold water.

"Jesus Christ!" Rick screamed, covering his genitals with his hands.

"It's for your own good," Lance said.

"God, you are a sicko." Rick slammed open the door and stalked out, grabbing our towel from on top of the toilet seat.

"It's a hot night in the big city, boy," Lance said. "You have to adapt. I'm adapting." He gave me a wicked smile. "So's Nadia here, aren't you? Our little Nadia is going to dance nude on Broadway. If that's not adapting to our sordid times, I don't know what is." He pinched my cheek. "Why else are we in the shower, if not to get wet? If you can't stand the water, get out of the shower!" He found this enormously funny.

Rick turned and pointed at Lance, looking at Alex. "This is what I'm talking about. See?" He was breathing heavily, the effects of the dope totally negated by the surprise glacial shower. Alex, unfazed by the cold water and the arguing around her, stepped out regally and pulled on her jeans, following Rick out of the bathroom. She didn't look back at Lance. Lance sighed and slumped to the floor of the shower, putting his head between his legs and covering his face with his hands. He was crying. He really loved Alex and knew she was going.

I left, scurrying naked across the floor because Rick had taken my towel. Everything was quiet, breaths held in. Even traffic in the street seemed to be waiting for the next move. Lance dressed and slammed out of the apartment, and so now there was no reason for secrecy and tiptoeing. I joined Alex and Rick in the kitchen. It was time to make travel plans. *Our* travel plans. I smiled at them, and after a polite second to acknowledge any hurt feelings I might have, they smiled back.

"I knew you would be pleased," Alex said.

"We'll call the moment we're settled," Rick said. He ran his hand through Alex's hair, delighting in the turn of luck that enabled him to do that.

Alex smiled then she laughed. I could hear her paper heart rustling and I briefly pitied Rick, because he was about to find out how little warmth that organ provided. But still they were deserting me and I was angry at both of them.

"Call?" My smile was feeble.

They kissed me relentlessly. "It's easier," Alex said.

"I can't stay here! Lance doesn't even like me!" I wondered what happened to Rick's belief that I should get out of there because Lance was evil. Only a minute ago he'd called him a sicko. Would they leave me with a sicko?

"Just use your charm on him. I know he'll succumb," Alex said. I knew then that she knew about me and Lance and she was paying me back. Still, I had only slept with him once. I didn't abscond with him in the middle of the night. "It's just until we get settled."

Alex took nothing more than a cloth backpack into which she threw some bottles. Shampoo mostly. Hair was definitely king in those days. Long beautiful hair. Rick stuffed some underwear into his guitar case and they were gone. They left with no more fanfare than that. I didn't ask where they were going. So besotted were they with each other, they wouldn't have understood the question. Assuming they even heard me.

I was left alone with my futon on the floor, that grimy mugginess you get only in a summer city filling my pores and numbing any resolve to just bolt, get the hell out of there. But it was more than that. You see, I had nowhere to go.

A few hours later, Lance came in. He wasn't alone. I heard some squealing and knew that a model wannabe was betting that Lance was what he claimed to be: a photographer who could jump-start her career after, of course, he'd jumped her. He came over to my futon and saw me.

"Jesus Christ," he muttered, obviously disappointed to find the wrong end of the dyad still there. Any mileage he had hoped to get out this woman in terms of jealousy from Alex was lost. He didn't waste time on preliminaries, but conducted business with his date.

I lay still, blocking out the sounds beyond the beaded curtains with the loud sounds of my own plans, which soon tangled with other night noises of New York until I could no longer distinguish which despair belonged to me and which belonged to those unseen others.

Chapter Five

From that moment, the summer assumed a new form. Whereas before I had yearned for an indefinite future with unnamed pleasures and glories, I now had a purpose, which was to get Alex back before I drowned in obscurity.

We, that is, Lance and I, settled into a routine. He didn't throw me out, as I expected, but allowed me space on my mattress. After that first night, he no longer brought women back to the loft, so I found some peace in that fragile area of my psyche. Within days our silent routine was forgotten and we began speaking like mad, mostly about our plans to get Alex back. That's all we could talk about. Did I think that this was a temporary fling? Did he think she had changed since he met her? When was I going to see her again?

Because I did see her. I wasn't exiled from her life as Lance, in his unfortunate status of ex-lover, had been. I was still her sister and you have to do something heinous to create a barrier between sisters. I went by her place every morning on my way to work, hoping to catch her. She never called me. Her new apartment was pretty big, even though I told her I thought she could afford much more.

"We don't want to get heavily into debt. We want to be free to leave. Anytime." She looked dreamily around. The apartment, while spacious, was stingily furnished. A waterbed, an electric-cable spool for a coffee table. A few boxes with clothes hanging out as if they were planning to escape in the middle of the night without paying the back rent. It was the way I had envisioned my life. It was *my* apartment, *my* life.

I think that was the first time I ever felt anything like hatred toward her. She was stealing the life I'd planned for us and using it all up herself. Hadn't I done all the planning? And now she was leaving me behind. I expected that from everybody else on the planet, but not Alex. I'd convinced myself that our love was a constant, the one immutable force in a bewilderingly inconstant universe. There was such a holy aura around peace and love back then, I didn't figure out 'til much later that love is the most self-serving of all emotions, having nothing whatever to do with altruism or reciprocity.

So, I saw Alex, but I only managed to catch her on her way to somewhere else. Her career was blasting off. She was in print and billboard ads for whiskey and cigarettes, usually as part of a party scene. Drinking a whiskey sour in an ad in Newsweek that I was scanning during a lull in button store commerce. Smoking a cigarette on a billboard on Houston Street. It always made me laugh because in real life she wouldn't touch either of them because they would wreck her face and here she was shilling as if they were the secret to her good looks.

And, of course, in Lance's apartment. There was no surcease to the burgeoning temple to Alex that Lance's apartment had become. He printed every frame he had ever taken of her. The blow-ups became bigger, the overlaps between them less tidy. We dined with our plates set on the out takes, sat on pieces of her lovely face enlarged to grotesque superhuman size. We spoke of her in the hushed tones of church. She had left us. She was always with us.

Zealot that I was I still imagined Alex wasn't lost to me completely and prepared for her return. I found a pattern of dishes, since she had unaccountably developed a taste for domesticity, in Macy's. I would walk across town on the way home from work to shoplift a few pieces.

The first night I walked around with a plate, pretending to examine it under better light in a different part of the store, near the women's dressing room on the second floor. The store dick, a middle-aged man with the raw skin of a redhead, was wise to me at once. When I turned around to nonchalantly slip the plate into my book bag, he was watching me. He tipped his hat back, interested, but instead of running, I made myself stay calm and sashayed into the dressing room, leaving the curtain flipped up over the pole and looked him coolly in the eye over the rack of woman's skirts that separated us. While he watched, I took off my shoes, then my socks and blouse. Finally, I pulled off my jeans and panties. I could see his face, poking up above the racks of sweaters and skirts, turning purple, then red, finally white and shuddering as I performed my languorous strip. I didn't have any problem making up a dance at the end. My nude *pas de deux*.

I enjoyed watching his misery behind the skirts and every day I added new flourishes to my act just to watch him cave, to lose all self-respect and possibly his job, for the pleasure of seeing me strip. I performed my dance until I had a complete set, wishing I had the nerve to do on stage what I didn't mind doing for Macy's house detective.

They were display pieces I told Lance when he asked me how the hell I could afford Lenox.

"Don't you think Alex would want some dishes that weren't touched by every bum in New York?" he asked meanly.

I remembered Alex laughing at the other things I had bought for her and felt a helpless rage, which I sought to quell by throwing a plate a Lance. It shattered on the cabinet behind his head. He grinned wickedly and tapped the top of his head as if to reassure himself it was still there, but went back to examining some proof sheets under a magnifying glass without saying a word. I took a walk trying to subdue my heart, which was about to explode. It took me an hour, just to be able to breathe again. When I got back to the apartment, Lance was gone.

We were always taking walks to avoid one another. I started walking west, trying to see what the rest of the city was like, trying to see if the party continued elsewhere. I walked past the art school, Cooper Union, through New York University and about twenty blocks later, at noon, I found myself on a West Village street whose store windows were filled with black leather jackets, studded wrist bands, and other assorted sexual weaponry. Shirtless men dressed in leather chaps and jock straps lolled in front of them. It was so different from Samaria, where we had known only one openly gay boy, who was forced to skulk around searching for like souls and finally, in his unhappiness, saw a shrink who told him he had until sundown to get out of town before he called the cops. There'd clearly be no cop-calling around here. Everyone was overtly on the prowl. A month ago there had been a riot at a big gay bar on Christopher Street and now being gay was a political fuck-you. One bearded man, dressed as a fairy princess, roller skated circles around passers-by. At first I thought he was panhandling, but as he rolled by, backwards, facing me, his chiffon ballerina skirt sweeping shag carpet hairy legs, I saw that he didn't have a container for money. He only wanted exactly what I was giving him: ten seconds of strict attention. After he got it, he skated on without a smile to the next person. Extracting his toll from everyone.

It was on one of my forays into the West Village that I saw our brother John. He was walking with another man on West 4th Street, their heads close together, the sunlight between their faces barely visible. I stepped quickly into a doorway, waiting until he passed, but I don't think it mattered because I was invisible to him. He could see only his companion. I turned around and watched them, jealous and in awe of their open affection.

Although I swear he didn't see me then, he tracked me down, arriving unannounced after I came home that night from the button store. He flipped an announcement of his upcoming show on the kitchen counter. His art was the daring kind popular then, although more of a curiosity now. He used bodies, not only his, rather than a brush to apply the paint.

"A show already?" I asked. "What are you doing, sleeping with the gallery owner?" The address was on Prince Street and from my walks in that neighborhood I knew that there were no art galleries there. It probably was some kind of garage gallery. That area of the city was all for rent and for sale signs, and spur of the moment music and art events were staged in the absence of legitimate tenants.

John laughed, looked around the loft, and seeing nothing *but* Alex on the walls, on the seats, on the tables, asked, "Where's Alex?"

He didn't seem alarmed when I told him she had "run away" with a musician. "She always had a soft spot for musicians," he said, casually telling me that he'd stopped to stare at a model's face on a poster for a fashion event, wondering if it was hers. "Anyway, it's hardly running away when you're in the same city," he pointed out, and to my irritation at his complete lack of understanding of the situation, he said it didn't qualify as running away when it was only your sister you were leaving.

"Not just sister," I said, trying to up the ante, give her betrayal more weight. "Her boyfriend, too."

"Boyfriends," he said, smiling. "I know about those."

I wanted to ask him about being gay, but I didn't dare. Despite the leather chaps and jock straps I saw on beautiful boys in the West Village, I was still ingrained with the Samarian view that being gay was something that was better done in secret. Anyway, we didn't have the words to talk about it then. It wasn't until I held his bony wrist fifteen years later, feeling him die, telling me of endless bath-house-body-part sex, of lovers whose lust was stoked with violence, trying to make sense of his yearning to be loved at any price, even the cost of his own life, that I learned how similar our souls were.

He smiled now and pulled a brown bottle from his jeans pocket and tapped out a few green and black capsules. "Just to help you relax. Nadia, get mellow. You can't go through life riding the back of a blade." He went to the sink and filled one of the margarita glasses Lance had brought back from Mexico. He held it out to me. I waved him off and he threw a handful of pills in his mouth and chased them down with a swig of water. He rolled a joint, which we were enjoying when Lance came in. John offered him a hit, which Lance not only took, but kept for himself. John abruptly left, giving me a kiss and protective pat, eyeing Lance warily. Lance and I stared at each other until we heard the gates of the elevator close.

"What's with the macho bullshit?" I asked.

"He's a fairy."

"Yeah, so?"

"You becoming a fag hag now?" Lance asked, noting the time of the opening of John's show, probably wondering if Alex would be there, if she had a connection to this man. He finally pushed the brochure off the table and into the waste paper basket.

"He's our brother," I said.

"No kidding?" Lance said. He picked the brochure out the wastepaper basket and read it again. "Another prettier sister."

I picked up the half full glass John had put down on the table and threw it at Lance, hitting him on the shoulder. It crashed to the ground, but the damned thing didn't break. It bounced.

"Cheap sonnofabitch glasses," I said, coolly, before noticing that Lance was coming at me, his eyes cold blue marbles.

"What? What?" I went to the other side of the table. "It didn't break," I said. I pointed to where the ugly glass lay. "See for yourself, it didn't break." I had never seen Lance angry.

He followed me around the table, holding his hands together as if to restrain himself from killing me. "Those are Alex's glasses," he said. "I got them for her. And they're going to be here when she comes back."

"She hated the fucking things," I said. "They're ugly and she hates them."

He shoved me against the kitchen sink. If he wanted to kill me then, he probably could have. Instead he began kissing me with his eyes closed. Roughly.

My heart was pounding the same way it was the night I threw the plate at him and had to go for the walk so I wouldn't blow up. I felt totally at the mercy of some foreign chemical that had hijacked my normal calm.

"Stop it," I said, "Stop it!"

I tried to remind myself that I hated this man, but this wasn't about hatred any more than it was about love. I tried to pound him off. Then I gave in. I closed my eyes and began kissing him back.

Chapter Six

So sultry nights drifted into mornings where a tang in the air teased me that my misery might end with the summer. Although I didn't linger too long on that reassurance. Part of the pleasure of youth is the complete conviction that no one has suffered as much or with as few uncaring witnesses.

Lance and I fought every night then made love, if you could call it that. It was almost a game where the rules changed nightly and the stakes grew increasingly frightening. And thrilling. I would instigate a fight and Lance would at first ignore me, then he would slap me, hard, trying to shut me up. If I cried, he would hit me again. He began to take off his belt and whip me with the smooth side, little welts formed up and down my backside. Once he tied me to the coffee table with it. Another time he gagged me with the belt to stop my screams. Or moans. Even now, I can't tell you which they were.

These were the only times we didn't talk about Alex, but she was there. Her photos loomed over on us like the statues of saints in a church. Once, when Lance threw me to the floor and I accidentally smashed my head on the end of the coffee table, I swooned and thought I was a sacrifice in a cult mass.

Gradually, the nightly dope parties stopped, whether because the people who came really were friends of Alex and Rick's, or because they saw nothing in either me or Lance to warrant return visits. I don't know. Dr. Lombardi, who it turned out was an actual friend of Lance's, came by once, saw my face, puffy from a battering, and got the hell out of there lest he be accused of being an accessory to domestic violence.

"I have enough shit to worry about," he apologized. Although I didn't think he actually *did* anything with his days, he claimed to have a rich work life. He was just one of those people, common then, who lived on other people's sofas and exchanged the largesse of their dinner companionship for a supply of pharmaceuticals.

Shel in the button store was startled the first time I showed up with lips bruised and swollen. He peered closely into my face, looking for a confession or a plea for help. Something. He gripped my forearm tightly, holding me until I would look at him. I shook him off.

"I fell," I said, unconvincingly.

Shel was pulled between absolute indifference to me and humanitarian compassion. On the one hand, he'd lost interest in me weeks ago when he realized that a youth army wasn't following in my wake, and if he came out of his back room at all it was just to sigh sadly and retreat. Only his Talmudic sense of loyalty kept me employed, because you didn't have to be an accountant to know I was a losing investment.

He never forced anything out of me. Domestic abuse then wasn't the *cause célèbre* it would become, and people felt it was none of their business if a husband or lover landed a few punches on a spouse. And anyway, how could I tell him that the blows weren't anything I didn't want? How could I tell him the pain was welcome because it was the only way I felt anything at all? The only time someone was paying attention to me.

Shel gave me an unasked-for raise of ten dollars a week, holding up his hand to fend off my thanks. Fending off explanations of where I got my bruises. It was hush money.

Rick was never around when I visited them. "Practicing," or "At a gig," Alex said. His career as a sessions musician was ramping up. A lot of the rock stars in those days were charismatic performers who needed backup musicians to make them sound, well, musical. Rick was in increasing demand. She handed me two tickets to a music festival in upstate New York. Three days of music and art, the tickets read.

"Who am I supposed to take?" I asked.

"Anybody you want," she answered indifferently. Her self-possession was maddening. She and Rick had formed a protective shell around themselves that allowed no one else in. Alex and I had had that once. But theirs was sealed with the sticky stuff of sex, which hardened like shellac.

"How am I supposed to get there?"

"Anyway you can."

Lance, would you be my date to Woodstock? I laughed thinking of us on anything like a date. What we had was so beyond a date. Dating was for children and the white gauze of a David Hamilton girlhood. We had even stopped eating. I had lost the ten pounds that everyone thought was keeping me from beauty, plus more. Once, in the middle of our games as Lance called what we did, someone knocked on the door, but we didn't open it. We froze, waiting for the clank and moan of the old elevator cables. I laughed, imagining the reaction, if they could see us, of whoever was behind that door until Lance slapped me back into our reality. I had finally become world-weary, but it had taken on an unspeakable aspect. I couldn't even tell Alex. I was hoping that she wouldn't notice my face, because I didn't know what I would tell her, but then I was pissed that she didn't, because I wanted her to know that in one area, at least, I was superior. That's how I felt. I was experiencing something she never would. I took the tickets.

"We'll see you there," she said, shutting the door behind me.

I did go to John's opening, at 96 Prince Street. His paintings, bold swatches of primary colors smeared on gigantic stretched canvases, had price tags of thousands of dollars for each one. I would have to work a whole year at the button store to afford even one of them.

He steered me to the table where the wine was being poured. "It's all a head game. The more elemental the painting the more you have to charge to be taken seriously."

"No offense, bro," I said, "but I could do this."

Instead of being insulted, John laughed, obviously delighted with his turn of fortune. A little red dot was attached to the square titles next to every painting. John's paintings were sold out. The boy who didn't go to his high school prom was a smashing success in New York City.

John was dressed all in black. A man dressed exactly like him came up shyly behind him and touched John gently on the small of the back with an index finger. John grabbed it without looking and held on for a moment before turning him around to introduce us.

"Glenn's a dancer," John said.

"Ahh, a dancer." It was the same man I had seen John with on the street. Could they be in love? I had become accustomed to the physical aspects of male love because between the leather jock straps and chaps and porn shops I had seen in the West Village there wasn't much left to imagine. But the idea of two men being *in love* intrigued me, just because I had never considered it.

John told me our father had written him a letter and he wanted to come to New York to see his children. The idea appalled me. I'd begun to think of myself as a creation that sprung out of the head of some major god instead of slogging my way down a mortal's birth canal. And the idea of my father—Dickie work pants, black lunch pail, neck crooked upwards as he looked for his children in the lofty regions of the city instead of the curbs where they actually dwelled— broke my heart. Would he want to film us now?

When the gallery was almost empty, the building owner who'd consented to give the show for a piece of the profits told us he had a surprise he wanted to share. He locked the doors and gestured for the dozen of us still there to ride to the 5th floor in the freight elevator. Then we followed him through a trap door onto the roof.

He stripped off his clothes, climbed a wooden ladder up the side of the old wooden slatted water tower, and without looking down on us disappeared off the side with a splash. He hoisted himself out of the water and gestured for us to join him. It took several stunned beats for it to register that in an act of improvisational urban genius he'd converted this giant utilitarian rain tank into a swimming pool. We cheered, stripped, clambered up, and dove in.

An hour later, drip dried and stoned on our host's grass, my brother's beau Glenn, before he and John left for party's unknown, gave me the name of professional theatrical pancake make-up that would cover my "battle scars," as he put it, better than the "pussy Maybelline stuff" I had been using.

I hung around downstairs, sucking down all the wine I could and snorting some guy's coke, informing the stragglers that I was the artist's sister.

A man wearing a beret and black turtleneck, claiming to be a painter handed me a scrap of paper with his phone number and his alleged name: a symbol of a star.

"Call me," Star said. He pointed to my face and I wasn't sure which intrigued him, my acne or black eye. "We'll get that down on paper."

The party moved to somebody's nearby loft and I went home. Instead of visiting Alex the next day, I tried to peek through the curtain of Star's front door as I rang his doorbell. He answered in a silk smoking jacket, the kind men wear in old movies, and no pants.

"I met you last night," I started to say in case he'd forgotten who I was.

He held up his hand to silence me and led me up to the third floor where he left me standing by a little table, which held a bell, a crystal decanter of whiskey and one glass, while he disappeared behind a thick black Chinese curtain. The room was lined with worn Chinese carpets and smelled of feet. I noticed that Star had taken off his shoes before vanishing, so I did the same.

I didn't hear any noise from behind the curtain, so I sat down and poured myself a whiskey. The glass itself was heavy and got weightier with each of the subsequent refills to which I helped myself. After I had poured myself a fourth and was starting to get bored with both the alcohol and foot odor, I decided to ring the bell which was apparently what he was waiting for. He appeared at the curtain, motioning for me to proceed into the studio, which was lined with portraits that were smudgy and hastily done. The only word that came to mind was "gibberish." Star was busy with something behind the easel, and I looked around for my seat, and seeing none, finally just lay down on the thickly carpeted floor.

"Is this right?" I asked self-consciously, turning around so he could get a better look at my butt, thinking he might want to paint my beautiful side.

Star shrugged. I spun around on one foot like a ballerina. "How about that?"
He didn't answer, so I danced some more, trying to get a reaction from him. I took off some of my clothes, but it didn't affect his wild gestures at the canvas. Finally, I removed all my clothing and closed my eyes and danced. After an hour or so of squirting paint and lurching forward with his palette knife, he sat down heavily on the rug, rubbing his eyes with his thumb and forefinger and gestured blindly with the other that I should leave.

I tried to sneak around him to get a glimpse of the canvas he had been painting on, but his body was like a barricade. His smoking jacket had fallen open to reveal that Star wore nothing underneath and that his talents were authentically gigantic in at least one area. He had one of the biggest reputations in New York my brother told me later. I paused, charmed by the sight, and his penis, like a child acting up for attention, proceeded to grow and dance towards me. I couldn't take my eyes off of it, thinking, "I did that."
"That's great," I whispered and Star opened one eye.

"Do you want to see?" He wrapped the smoking jacket tightly around himself and got up to turn the easel so I could see the painting.

My reward was a look at the canvas which was "only a beginning" he begged when I freaked out, and "you can't make any sense of it at this stage." The painting showed none of the physical wounds I was scared of having revealed to the world. But all of the emotional ones. It was as if I were skinned alive and the hollowness inside revealed. How could he see all that?

I have since learned that the one unforgivable sin is for someone to lend you the glasses through which they view you. Unless they are in love with you, the view is never as flattering or as interestingly evil as you imagine and the most you can hope for is that you don't look like an ass. It took loud persuading for me even to consider returning for the completion of my portrait. His wife, Sally, a Philadelphian Main Line matron who had sold the family china and jewelry to support Star's career, came out of *nowhere* (Jesus, was she watching me from behind one of these creepy hanging carpets?) to cajole me with the promise that my fame as Star's model would be as great as his if I just stuck it out. I left for the button store with a big "maay-bee" and the promise of fame swirling through my greedy soul.

That afternoon, Rick came by. It was the first time I had seen him since he'd left with Alex. He wore Alex's presence. She made everyone she was connected with appear more than they were. Even Rick seemed less scurvy rock musician and more romantic figure now that he was imbued with Alex's aura.

"You're looking well," I told him busying myself with the bric-a-brac display for Back-to-School. There is bric-a-brac to celebrate every event in the human condition. For Back-to-School, it's mostly plaid ribbons.

"You look like shit," he said. He grabbed me by the shoulder and made me turn around. "What the hell is that sicko doing to you?"

I looked him fully in the face, letting him get a good look. It amused me to think that he thought I was being taken advantage of, when the truth was that most of the time I was the one who started things. "What's it to you?" I asked.

It obviously didn't mean much because he quickly remembered what he came for and looked nervously at the curtain that separated us from Shel. "I need to talk to you," he said.

I folded my arms over my chest. "So talk."

"I mean, is he cool?" he jerked his head towards the back room.

"Well, he's not deaf, if that's what you mean, but I doubt if he gives a damn about anything you have to say."

"It's about Alex."

I felt my neck stiffen, but forced my breath to go in and out regularly.

When he saw I wasn't responding, he said, "We want to make it legal."

"You mean get married?" I almost shouted, looking over my shoulder to see if Shel was standing in the doorway.

Rick smiled. "Yeah. Sis." He punched me playfully on the arm. I winced and not just because he hit on a particularly sore patch of welts.

"You can't do that. She's not ready. She's too young. We're just starting out. We haven't even begun to live. She can't be tied down to you." I was rambling, trying to stall, to give him as well as me a good reason why this marriage couldn't happen.

He looked less sure of himself. "She loves me," he said, unsteadily.

"No, she doesn't."

He shrugged. "We're going to London. I got some gigs lined up."

He continued on but I'd stopped listening. It wasn't true, I wanted to scream. I knew, of course, that Alex was infatuated with this boy. But I also knew that the infatuation would die, probably as quickly as it was born. She couldn't ever really love such an *ordinary* creature. Because, if she could, what did that make her?

What did that make *me*?

I caught a few words of his monologue. "So you see how it is," he was saying. "Do you have any ideas?"

"About what?"

"To square it away with the draft board. I can't get a passport with this thing hanging over my head. Alex says you're the smartest person she knows. She says you would know what to do."

He looked so miserable and innocent that for a moment I almost forgot that we were rivals. I felt benevolent because Alex had called me the smartest person she knew. Besides, I had no quarrel with American boys who didn't want to travel 10,000 miles to blow Vietnamese boys to smithereens. So on one level I really wanted to help him. But mostly I didn't.

"Did you ever even register?" I asked.

"Haven't been near a post office in six years," he said smugly then he looked sad.

"Lots of boys slip across the border to Canada." Of course, Canada wasn't where it was at for a musician. I envisioned Rick, with his dirty mane and skinny legs trying to outmaneuver British immigration who would laugh him right back across the ocean. They had their own supply of recalcitrant rockers. They didn't need to import more.

"It wouldn't be right to involve Alex in something like that. She deserves better than just being on the run."

He was right. She did deserve better than to slink through borders and give up a career in modeling to skulk around avoiding F.B.I. agents. Slipping into dark alleys, registering under phony names, wasting youth in fungous cellars. That was nothing at all like the life I had envisioned for us. I had to save her.

I patted Rick's arm in a sisterly way and told him I had some contacts and that maybe it wasn't as hopeless as it seemed, all the while thinking that this was the opportunity I had been waiting for. I finally had a plan. I would nail him. Pretend to help him, but lay a trap of government flunkies who would do the dirty work for me. It would be an easy win for them, a long-haired draft evader with a gee-tar. All they had to do was wave their guns around and bring the boy down, and out of our lives. It was simple. All I had to fill in were details. Alex would be mine again.

Rick, of course, couldn't know what I was thinking. He thanked me. I thought he was going to cry. I wondered that I had ever been lonely enough to go to bed with this person, because all I felt for him now was repulsion for his weakness. And pity for what I was about to do to him. He would have to be sacrificed to save Alex.

"You're going up to Woodstock, aren't you?" he asked.

"Woodstock? What's that?"

"Alex said she gave the tickets to you." He seemed hurt that I had forgotten his gift. He was playing back-up for some group.

"Oh yeah. The three days of music and art thing." It was more a statement than a question. I had no intention of going. I couldn't ask Lance and there was nobody else I knew, so small had my world become. I was in the middle of one of the biggest cities in the world and my orbit consisted of two, maybe three (if you counted my brother) people. To tell the truth, I had become so addicted to playing with Lance, as he called it, I couldn't stand to be away from it for three days of music, art, or anything else.

"I went to a lot of trouble to get those," he said. He then kissed my hand and left the store. I promised to call him that very evening.

I attacked the rest of the afternoon with renewed vigor. Suddenly, the button store didn't seem depressing. Or sordid, as Alex had pronounced it. It was a place of hope, of new beginnings. Wasn't Shel trying to make a new beginning with a veritable button renaissance? Weren't these teachers who were buying this crap for their classrooms merely trying to celebrate life and the passing of the seasons by festooning themselves and everyone around them in crepe paper and bric-a-brac? How could I have ever cynically dismissed them?

I copied the phone number of FBI headquarters from the yellow pages and slipped the paper into my pocket along with some onyx buttons I'd been admiring. I greeted all the customers with a politeness that was probably ordinary, but new for me. The customers looked surprised and wary, most had already been recipients of my sullen service, but soon they capitulated to my new self and smiled. Even Shel responded to the new vibe I'd introduced to the store by coming out from behind his curtain and rubbing his hands in delight.

With so little effort, I saw that I could make anyone happy. I'm ashamed to admit it had never occurred to me that I could use being nice for any sort of *good*. I only saw it as a colossal opportunity to help me get my own way.

I smiled and dispensed goodwill. Everyone my golden beams touched was happy. Everyone. Soon it would be me.

Chapter Seven

Later I learned we weren't the only ticket holders who didn't make it to Max Yasgur's farm in upstate New York. A whole platoon of festival-goers got diverted on the way, seduced by easier, more sensuous parties. And now, seeing the video and movies of that festival, the mud and mayhem, I am glad that Lance and I only made it as far as West Chester.

Of course, if I had made it to Woodstock, I may have found myself diverted from Lance, which in retrospect would have been a good thing. But we didn't. We stopped at White Plains and despite what happened there, we remained stuck together.

Lance laughed, as I knew he would, when I suggested that it would be nice to leave the city for a while. Breathe some wholesome air, eat some regular food. We had gotten caught in the spring roll, egg drop soup, coffee routine, when we remembered to eat at all, both of us looking the worse for it. I don't think we had any vitamins left in our bodies. It's funny to think of that now: *vitamins*. We had so much juice in our bodies I didn't believe we would ever dry up. No young person ever does. Alex, when she noticed me at all, did comment that I was looking older, which I took to mean that I was finally looking mature. She didn't seem alarmed, and she never mentioned the bruises that ringed my face like smudged charcoal, so I thought no more about it.

I have a photograph Lance took of me at that time. I was thin, which made me happy. The longed-for cheekbones had emerged from their jelly doughnut padding. My hair was turning wiry, unruly spikes stuck up from my normally straight dark hair when I remembered to comb it. My eyes had purple rings under them, diminishing somewhat the acne that raged despite lack of fuel. Lance had decided that I needed some cocaine to rev up my energy. Apparently, I was slowing down. I wasn't giving an acceptable amount of response, as Rick would put it.

Rick. I would deal with him when we returned from Woodstock, but he and Alex were never far from my mind.

Finally, Lance agreed we should go, and even said he knew some guys we could catch a ride with. I thought for a moment that maybe the company of other people would make us an official couple. Whatever that was. The only thing we had in common was our obsession with Alex, but we'd been together long enough that our perverse entanglement was forming a life of its own.

That Thursday night we headed out of the city in a Volkswagen bus with Lance's friends. They picked us up in front of our building, not honking because it would have gotten lost in the noise of the city, and not bothering to come to the door to tell us they were there because they were having fun smoking dope.

The bus was green and white. The back seats had been removed and replaced with a dilapidated love seat. For the first time in a week I felt my old optimism returning. We were going somewhere. On the road. Forward momentum.

The three guys who picked us up nodded at us with glazed passive eyes when we stood looking in through the windshield. I waved my ticket at the driver, a tall curly-haired guy named Teddy. He must have been at least 6'5" because his blond afro touched the ceiling of the bus. He had a cotton kerchief tied around his Harpo hair like an Indian headband. He didn't wear a shirt in order to better show off his slim, muscular build. His face was like a rodent's, with two rat-teeth getting caught on his lower lip, eyes gleaming orange where they should have been white. But I couldn't take my eyes off his body. Lance hustled me into the love seat, snorting.

"Don't be an asshole," he said, throwing my bag behind the seat.

"What asshole?"

"He's not your type."

I smiled at the guy anyway, showing him my ticket again as if I needed to prove I was legitimate. He nodded, bobbing to the Jethro Tull blaring from the radio. The guy in the passenger's seat was just as tall, but much better looking. He had dark hair and broad features that seemed almost American Indian, but he wasn't. He was Hungarian and his name was Arpad. His gleaming hair was cut straight across in bangs, accentuating a wide brow, cut cheekbones. His eyes were black. He laughed when he heard our exchange then kept on laughing at some stoned diversion.

"Everybody ready?" Teddy asked, looking at me in the rearview mirror, putting the bus in gear. His eyes didn't seem orange when they were focused on me.

"Onward," I said. God, I was so happy to be going someplace else. I tapped Teddy on his bare shoulder. "Could you turn that up?" I asked him, making a twisting motion with my fingers.

He nodded and turned the radio louder. "You got it, Mama."

Lance covered his ears then thought better of it and gave Teddy directions on getting out of the parking space.

"Too loud for you, Dad?" I asked.

Lance ignored me and continued bossing Teddy. "Cut it, cut the wheel now!"

A small guy was sitting on the floor in back with the bags. He was smoking a regular cigarette. He had a brown beard and a hillbilly hat. I smiled at him as an introduction and he offered me a Camel.

"Thanks."

Suddenly, there was a thud on the side of the vehicle, as if we had hit something. A familiar face pressed against the bus' window. His mouth was squashed flat, revealing everything you wanted to know about his dental history. Not a filling in his beautiful white teeth. He knocked on the window, forcing Teddy to stop, stalling the engine.

"Whaddafuck!" he said. He yanked on the emergency brake and turned the engine over, tying to escape the lunatic.

Lance however, opened the side door and let the Guru tumble in.

"Thanks, man," the Guru said, pulling up his filthy robes to climb over me and onto the love seat.

"Sonofabitch," he said, noticing me. "The whole family's here." He plucked the blue eye out of its socket, put it in his pocket, pulled his robes around him and began snoring. He had a pungent smell, like he'd foraged his dinner from a dumpster, and as he settled into a deep sleep, the odors that clung like a protective shield around his body were released to choke us.

The ride, despite complete incompetence with the road map and basic driving skills, was not unpleasant. The dope had made everyone mellow. Even Lance told a joke, the point of which I can't for the life of me remember now, but it was funny and he smiled at me for approval, and I have to admit, I smiled back. It may have been the only innocent thing we ever shared.

We had to make another stop, to "pick up a chick" somewhere in West Chester, and after getting lost for two hours before we even made it out of Manhattan, everyone decided to park it there for the night. We were having fun anyway.

The woman we picked up was Susan Artis. She was a big girl, big breasts, long legs, birthing hips. Her face, though, was delicate. It was made whiter by her dark curls and black eyes and Lance told me that her brain was fried. She had done too much acid and was given to tremors and sudden crying. "Sounds like a normal girl to me," I said. "No, no, it's the acid," Teddy said.
The men wanted to believe in the danger of dope so they could feel adventurous taking it.

She had modeled briefly in New York, but her voluptuous body couldn't maintain a waif-like appearance for more than a few days, and for that she had to fast for weeks. It was a hell of a tortuous way to make a living, and the only tangible she netted from the experience was a Physician's Desk Manual knowledge of drugs.

The part that made Susan interesting to me was that she had briefly been in involved with Rick before we met. She had, in fact, put him up in her family's apartment in New York City. It was her parents, returned unexpectedly from a trip, who had thrown him out the morning he was waiting for me in front of the button store. Rick the lady-killer.

Her parents weren't at their country house, they were in their apartment in the city, probably barricading the fort against the next wave of hippie intruders, and Susan asked me if I wanted to drop some acid and so we did. I had never done acid before and everyone made a big show of envying me my first time.

"It's always best the first time, because it hits you by surprise. You never suspect that there was all this neat stuff inside you," Arpad said. He told me he had done acid one hundred and twenty times. He was trying to train his brain so it wouldn't need any stimulation like acid, so that it would just kick into a cool grove on its own. It was the only time all weekend he spoke a complete sentence. I guessed it was the silent brain training.

Teddy, who had done acid only once himself and didn't like it, insisted on acting like a nursemaid, fixed us a batch of scrambled eggs and a container of Carnation's Instant Breakfast (chocolate) for nourishment. "You got to eat. Or you'll go bad in the middle of things."

"I heard of people jumping out of windows on acid, I never heard of anyone dying of starvation," I said, already feeling wobbly as the drug did its dragon walk down my spine, causing Teddy's face to get smaller and his body to become absurdly big. I laughed and fell back on the sofa. Susan rolled back next to me. Soon I forgot Susan as I watched the others file back and forth in front of us, trying to jimmy open Susan's parents' liquor cabinet. It was taking them an incredibly long time to do something so simple.

"For God's sake, open it!" I screamed. "Open it, open it, open it!"

The Guru had appeared by my side, stroking my head. I remember thinking he really smelled sweet. I didn't know why I found his odor so offensive in the bus. "Why can't they open it?" I started to cry.

"It's only juice darlin'" he said. "Juice heads will always find a way to get their juice."

Lance gave me a mean look from the living room door. He hadn't taken any acid. He didn't like to be that much out of control. I stuck my tongue out at him, but my tongue rolled out and out. It never stopped rolling out. I didn't have the energy to reel it back in. In exhaustion, I let it stay where it was, where people could use it as a carpet.

Susan had jumped up and was pulling me off the sofa. "We got to get outa here," she whispered dramatically.

I nodded and we slipped out the door while the others were occupied with the lock on the liquor cabinet. It was getting darker, with a "hint of rain," Susan kept repeating, like a mantra, kicking her shoes off, thumping the ground. "Hint of rain, hint of rain, hint of rain."

We followed a back road into the woods in our bare feet, the trees, satyrs from another world, teased me. Half-man, half-plant, their rough bark in sympathy with the ragged skin that housed me. The wind blew their branches towards me attempting an embrace. I felt adored. I reached back, lying down on the road, waiting for these giant creatures to take me. I remember laughing with happiness, and if it's possible to have an orgasm in your soul, I certainly had one then.

As suddenly as that sensation came, it left, leaving a void for reality to reenter. I became aware that it was more than hinting at rain now, it was pouring and we did the only sensible thing we could, we stepped onto the porch of someone's house. The house was a little off the road, painted white with red shutters, red and white geraniums on the windowsills. I laughed, thinking the owners had a great sense of humor to decorate with such a silly motif. The door to a two-car garage attached to the house was open. No cars were inside. We went into an enclosed porch. It wasn't locked and anyway we had the right to enter because one of us had decided no one could own property.

"What an absurd idea," I lectured, "that someone could actually own a piece of the earth that was given to everybody." I could hardly wait to get back to tell our friends. My thoughts had never been so lucid.

We snooped around the porch, which was set for dinner, for us! A round table covered with a red and white gingham tablecloth was set with five place settings. Through some sort of cosmic acid connection, the person who lived in this house was waiting for us. A Doberman Pincher crouched in the corner, but after investigating, he seemed unimpressed and lay back down, putting his head on his paws. I stared into his eyes, trying to remember why it was that you weren't supposed to look a dog in the eye—a sign of challenge to the dog's manhood or something—when Susan came out of the house, where she'd been looking around.

"Check this out," she commanded, going back inside.

I hesitated then figured what the hell. If you can't own the earth, you can't own a living room either or the logic breaks down. And everything seemed so logical to me, so self-apparent. I couldn't imagine what had been keeping me from seeing the truth before. I decided that acid was very good stuff indeed and I would do it as often as I could and get everyone else I knew to take it. Alex, for example. She should take a gallon to get her off of whatever weird trip she was on.

I was stuck outside the door, unable to engage my body while my mind was using up all this energy. Susan came out and dragged me into the living room, which was like stepping into a duck blind.

Decoys, all sizes and colors lined the floor like a platoon. There were even some that were big enough to sit on, which we did, riding around the room like we were toddlers on tricycles. On the ceiling paddling bird feet were stenciled, giving the disconcerting illusion that we were watching ducks swim overhead.

"Jesus," Susan said. She had a joint in her pocket, which she fired up and passed to me. "I got to mellow out a little bit. This duck thing is heavy."

"Yeah, heavy," I said. I couldn't escape the feeling that I was underwater and I found myself gasping for air. "Do you think the people who live here are cool?"

"Very cool," she answered.

We wandered into the kitchen and saw that someone had been preparing dinner. A chopped onion was on the cutting block, an uncooked carcass of some bird in a pan, and the radio was on, tuned to a station that was having a call-in vote on which group you liked better: the Stones or the Beatles. An open half-gallon bottle of Almaden Chablis was on the sink and a half-drunk glass of wine was next to the cutting board.

"What happened here?" I asked. It looked as if someone had been abducted right in the middle of fixing dinner.

"I'll bet really cool people live here," Susan said. "They didn't want to scare us, so they left to let us get acquainted with things."

"They're going to be so glad to finally meet us."

"So glad."

We debated whether or not to start cooking the duck ("You think they really eat ducks? Maybe it's a goose, or a mean ole chicken. I wouldn't mind eating a chicken.") and decided that we were too fucked up to do it right and would probably burn the place down, which we didn't want to do because we *liked* these people with their weird red, white and ducky thing, and we wanted them to like *us*, which they wouldn't if we burned down their house. Anyway, since no one could own anything, the place belonged as much to us as to the people who lived here full-time, so we didn't want to burn it down in case we came back to visit.

We hung around, waiting, for what seemed like hours in acid time, probably five minutes in elapsed time, before we got bored and decided to move on. Susan left the roach in an ashtray for them, finished off the wine in the glass and we headed out, back up the driveway. The Doberman got up to stretch and we waved good-bye to him.

We were at the point where the driveway met the road when a red Cadillac convertible with a white canvas top sped down the muddy path, almost knocking us down as it turned towards the house. Between the windshield wipers, we could see that the driver was a shriveled up woman with white hair, steel glasses and deep furrows between her eyebrows. She braked to get a better look at us and the Doberman started barking, clawing at the porch screen, suddenly mad to break out and tear us apart.

Susan and I grabbed hands and ran into the woods, until we collapsed against a tree, panting hard and laughing until unaccountably we started to cry. Susan had medicine for that, too. She pulled out some green and black capsules ("Librium will set you free, my dear"), and we opened our mouths for rainwater to wash them down. Every emotion had its antidote in a drug, and I began to see the possibilities of a life lived totally without wants or needs. Those minutes I spent in the woods with Susan Artis while the Librium liberated my soul were some of the happiest I have ever spent. For the life of me, I can't tell you what weird Puritanism keeps me, even now, from becoming a pill freak, letting their cool narcotic fingers soothe my overheated psyche.

Susan was a nice girl, which seems an odd appellation to pin on a girl who ingested every chemical and man she could corner. In my drugged state she seemed the pinnacle of mother earth warmth. And nice. So nice, in fact, that I told her everything about Alex and Rick and what I planned to do to them.

Susan wasn't surprised that Alex was my sister. She knew who Alex was, of course. "Yeah, you kind of look alike," she said, ignoring my welts and scary hair. I had as much similarity to Alex as a painting by Picasso has to its model, but for a while we accepted the fiction that I, too, was a great beauty. I had never talked to anyone about Alex before, especially not a girl, and it seemed like a betrayal, which I justified by saying that Alex was betraying me. She was supposed to be helping me achieve my (our) destiny, and she was deserting me for her own happiness.

Her black eyes narrowed in interest when she found out that Rick had deserted me for my lovelier sister.

"But what about you," I protested, "He deserted you" I squeaked out the last part, "For me!"

Susan shrugged, easy with the flow of men in and out of her life. It would never occur to her to punish one for abandoning her any more than she would expect retribution for doing the same. But she sensed that it wasn't so casual for me. I aroused her protective instincts. Women, I have found, can be ferocious defenders.

I lowered my head in fake despair. "It's not him I care about, it's Alex."

As solid as I felt my fledgling friendship with Susan at that moment, an hour later I was betrayed again as she told everything to Lance. I could tell by his easy laughter and mocking look towards me that he hadn't done any drugs, and I felt at a disadvantage as you do when your mind is the only one in chaos. But later, when we were alone, he said that Susan would be the perfect person to help us and I was right to tell her. Her parents had connections ("With, you know, real people. Her father is a lawyer") and they thought that Rick was a scurvy boy who had to atone for the sin of entering their daughter's life, a punishment that would keep him from being so bold again. Some time in Vietnam was just the ticket for a class crasher like Rick. The nerve of him, a blue-collar boy going around stealing women better than he deserved.

Teddy made a stew that had cooked too long on the stove and
burned. The meat itself was unidentifiable and I couldn't help
thinking of ducks—God, that seemed like weeks ago—so was glad it
was inedible. I started making pitchers of Carnation Instant
Breakfast, which the crew drank as fast as I could mix it. The Guru
had come out of whatever hole he had retreated to and drank too. In
truth, I was starving and wanted a glass myself, but I couldn't seem to
get at it, so quickly did everyone slurp up the brew.

We planned to get on the road first thing in the morning to get
to Woodstock. Teddy and Arpad checked out the map with initial
resolve, then later I saw them in the same position, smoking a joint,
the map in a heap at their feet.

The Guru spent a full hour in the master bedroom's shower,
steaming a month's worth of dirt off himself and inadvertently
steaming the pictures and wallpaper off the walls. It looked as if the
bathroom were melting. I couldn't be sure then how much of the
perceived destruction was the residual acid in my system and how
much was reality, but the next morning everyone was tiptoeing over
strips of sticky wallpaper on the floor.

Lance and I slept on the same bed, everyone assumed we would
because we were technically living together, I guess. But the truth
was, that after that first night, Lance and I had never actually *slept*
together. We would have our version of sex, then I retreated back to
my lair, the futon. We never shared anything as mundane as pillow
talk. I was trepidatious as he crawled in next to me, but I didn't
flinch as he hit me good-naturedly on the rump and told me that
enlisting Susan's help to get Rick was the best thing I had ever done.
The best thing. Her father was a lawyer. Did I know that? He began
a monologue about something or another, when I dozed, the acid
making me dream of shrubbery suddenly sprouting legs and walking
off of lawns. The owners couldn't get their hedges to stay put as the
bushes ran amok in blind circles. Beating the shrubs with sticks didn't
help as they had no nerve endings, and trying to talk reason to them

didn't help as they had no ears. I laughed aloud and Lance woke me to ask what was so damned funny.

At three o'clock, we were awakened by a loud knock on the door that turned out to be Susan's cousin, a hippie from Florida who made belts. He traveled with his wife, a large dark haired woman in a red muumuu and a two-year old boy, naked except for a nautical cap that said, "Captain Gerber." They too were on their way to Woodstock. We stayed up the rest of the night talking, groovin on how cool we discovered each other to be, discussing the best routes to get there. Everyone had an opinion about it, which seemed stupid because it wasn't as if there were a lot of choices in the matter, just find Route 87. The meatier part of the discussion was more about how to get out of town without arousing suspicions in the local constabulary, because among us there must have had two pounds of drugs. With long hair and trails from old trips streaming from the back of Volkswagen busses we might as well have worn a bullseye.

Around seven o'clock they set up their tent on the front lawn and everyone went to sleep, passed out until the middle of the afternoon. By then, of course, after coffee, cigarettes, some stale cinnamon buns for Captain Gerber, everyone was hungry, so Susan and I took the Captain shopping at the local Shop Rite. She showed me how to shoplift cigarettes, by taking the carton off the shelf, ripping out the bottom end and slipping the packs into her waiting woven Greek bag. I was changing Captain Gerber's diaper on a closed check-out lane, causing every available employee to come over to chastise me, while Susan slid plastic wrapped steaks in her bag, topped it off with red potatoes and sashayed out the front door, nonchalantly picking up a newspaper on the way out.

Susan and I made dinner. The guys rolled joints. Lance told me that Susan had been in touch with her father and that the "wheels were in motion to get that sonofabitch, Rick, or whatever his real name is. It's not even his goddamned real name. Do you know that? Not even his goddamned real name."

After toking up, no one was motivated to get in the vans and go anywhere, so we smoked some more and swatted away mosquitoes, despite Arpad's insistence that smoking marijuana produces a chemical in the skin that repels insects. Or maybe it was LSD, he said, as we scratched ourselves raw. It probably was the LSD, because none of the pests were bothering him. He must've had enough acid in his system to "kill every mosquito in the Keys" as Susan's cousin said. Everyone decided that they needed immunity, too, and Arpad passed around tabs of White Lighting as if it were insect repellent and we began the day all over again from a different perspective. There was no more talk of going to Woodstock, as we spent the remainder of the weekend immobilized. Like a miracle, no more mosquitoes bothered us and we considered founding a new religion based on it, but like other drug-induced great ideas, the notion was downgraded to a joke when the drugs wore off.

I have to say in the middle of all this, that I felt for the first time that my life was taking off, that perhaps I didn't need Alex to take me into another world. I was in another world and, in my way, I was having a great time. My need to get Rick in order to get Alex back, didn't seem quite so desperate. I had actually spent a weekend thinking of something other than her. I even broached it with Lance, that perhaps we ought to forget the whole thing. Or at least put it off and let the romance die of natural causes.

"Are you crazy?" he asked. "That's the drugs talking, not you." The only thing he had imbibed all weekend was Susan's parent's scotch. He seemed put off by my sudden lack of passion for our joint pursuit, so I wasn't surprised later when I heard sounds coming out of Susan's bedroom, the door was open, and I could see him balling her. Susan wasn't doing it for anything other than the fact that it was her nature to fuck any man who asked her to. But Lance was too vocal, and he never made any noise, so I knew he was making sure that I discovered the price of my desertion.

"Anyway," Lance told me later, as he toweled off from his afternoon tryst, "It's too late. Susan's father hates him more than you ever could. Rick screwed his little girl."

"And that would make you what?" I asked.

He ran the towel between his buttocks, like a pipe cleaner. "It doesn't matter what the hell I am. We're getting Alex back. The wheels are in motion. There's no turning back."

Chapter Eight

The cousins from Florida packed up their tent, Captain Gerber
helping by banging each pole with a stick before his father packed it
away, everyone waving as their van pulled away and made the left
turn south, towards home.

The rest of us jammed our belongings back in our bus, but it was
like putting the stuffing back in a baseball. It was springy and mushy
and I didn't see how all this junk, as well as ourselves, was going to
fit. I stayed outside rather than confront the bigger mess we had left
inside. Besides the stripped bathroom, we had broken the doors on
the liquor cabinet to get at the booze, and had thrown a pound of
half-cooked spaghetti on the wall to see if it was finished cooking as
someone had seen Jack Lemmon do in a movie. Those were the
obvious crimes. If we had looked closely we would have noticed
other things, like wine stains on the Oriental carpets and salad
dressing on the sofa, but we didn't fine-tune the inspection that
much. The guys tried to tidy up, but they didn't have the radar for
details and so after spending a good amount of time staring at our
mess, if not actually doing anything about it, we squeezed into the
bus and drove back home.

Susan had caught a train to the city early that morning, so she
couldn't supervise the clean-up crew and give her seal of approval.
More importantly to me, I didn't see her to discuss the details of our
plan about Rick. I figured she would just forget it, and part of me, at
least, was relieved. It was all right to talk about involving the law in
our lives, but to actually invite the law in seemed traitorous and risky,
considering the volume of illegal chemicals that fueled our lives.

Shel had seen Woodstock on the news that weekend and was proud that I was part of such a wholesome, youthful happening.

"Just having fun, right?" he asked me, putting an arm around my shoulder the minute I walked in the button store. "Just kids having fun. Did you have fun?"

He beamed at me, checking for fresh bruises and, finding none, widened his smile. "The fresh air, the friends. It's nice for you, I think. What you need." Happy that I done something positive for myself, Shel showed me what he had done for me: he had rearranged the store so that the exotic buttons were in the back, the bric-a-brac was moved towards the front with a whole new section devoted to craft supplies. He had even made a small concession to the craze (as he put it) for zippers, allowing Talon to put up a small rotating stand with seven and nine inch zippers in beige, white and black.

"It's time to change, I think," Shel said, putting his hands on his belly, rubbing it enthusiastically. "Why was I hanging on to an old way of thinking? I saw the Woodstock on the television and I think, young people are the future. If they don't want buttons, why should I try to sell them buttons? Sell the young people what they want!" He went on talking like this for a few minutes, swirling the zipper rack then stopping it suddenly like a kid with a whirligig, giving me instructions on the new inventory, how best to pitch it to customers, before he wandered away behind the plastic curtain to his office.

Shel had made other improvements over the weekend, too. A new coffeepot, white with a timed wake-up and grind function had replaced the old. I poured a little into my cup and sipped, rolling the warm brew around my tongue waiting for a taste that didn't come, it was so weak.

Business was slow. It was August and any New Yorker who had the means had left the city for either beach or mountains. Someplace cool. I told this to Shel, but it didn't stop his fretting. He had made quite an investment in the new stock and wanted to see it pay off immediately. No, he hadn't taken out a loan or anything like that, he said. He just had an accountant's desire to see numbers march smartly from the debit column to the credit side of the ledger. That was nothing I could relate to, so I sat on a stool in the middle of the craft section, reading the paper and periodically taking a piece of red felt off the shelf to wipe the perspiration from my neck and face. The place was boiling. I left early to relieve some of the financial strain on Shel and walked to see Alexandria and Rick.

The last time I had seen them I had said I was working on getting fake papers for Rick, to get him out of the country. So I was surprised to be treated like a celebrity when I arrived. Alex opened the door, clasping me in an embrace. Rick was right behind her, trying to wiggle into the hug.

"He was here today," Alex said. "The man took down all sorts of information about Rick and said he would take care of everything. I told you, didn't I?" Alex looked at Rick, triumphantly. He'd obviously doubted my ability to come through on a promise. I felt miffed that he would underestimate me then contrite when I remembered I had actually done nothing at all and Rick's assessment, rather than Alex's, was the more accurate.

"What man?" I asked.
"He was a lawyer. He's going to help Rick. Give him some papers that say he's exempt from military service. I told you," Alex said to Rick.
They were set up for a party. Paper plates and cups were on the table. Big jugs of wine and chips.

"More food's coming later," Alex said. "We were going to call you."

I opened a bag of chips and began nibbling nervously. "Do you know when?" I asked.

Alex was rummaging in the refrigerator and looked back at me. "I was going to call you as soon as I thought you would be home from work."

"No, I mean, do you know when they are going to have the papers for Rick?"

The man hadn't said, but their opinion was it was imminent. I left, telling them to call as soon as it was party time. Alex took my hand, "Nadia, I don't know what we would have done without you. It seemed so hopeless."

"Nothing's ever hopeless," I said, wresting my hand away.

The Guru was back on duty in the hallway. He laughed when he saw me, in a comfortable way, not his usual mockery, and didn't deter me as he usually did, with either his strength or wit. I stepped lightly over him and the olive pits he was spitting on the stairs.

Lance was developing pictures from the weekend, he said. I hadn't been aware that he was even taking them. When he went out later that evening, I opened the darkroom to look through them. They were lewd pictures of Susan. It must have been after their bout in the bedroom. I wondered if Susan had been aware that he was taking them, she was so drugged. It didn't seem sporting. I snatched up the prints, about to destroy them, when I thought to look for the negatives. They weren't there. They weren't anywhere. I remembered the locked briefcase I had rummaged through the first week I was alone in the apartment. I found it in the bottom of his supply cabinet, exactly where it was before. It was still locked, but it was only a briefcase, the easiest locks in the world to pick, and soon I was in, shuffling through images of strangers in intimate, if slightly unnatural, poses.

Then, at the bottom of the pile, images of a woman who looked a lot more familiar: Alex. I found it hard to both see and breathe, the pounding blood flooded my chest and head. When I could focus again, I shook the briefcase upside down, looking for negatives. They weren't there. I upset the entire darkroom looking for negatives. He obviously didn't keep them there. The only negatives I found were those in innocent poses, girls mugging for fashion spreads, labeled politely with the date of the shoot and the girl's name.

The phone call from Alex came at ten.

"They got him first," she sobbed into the phone.

I could barely understand her, and I willed myself to act normally, pretending that that I didn't know that the lawyer who'd interviewed Rick worked for Susan's father. "Alex, slow down, honey. What's the matter?"

"The FBI got to him. He's on a bus right now to South Carolina."

"Already?" I marveled at how quickly the law acted. "For what?"

"They said if he went right away and quietly, they wouldn't press charges. He's going to basic training, then to infantry training and from there..." She couldn't go on.

"Don't move, Alex. I'll be right over."

"Don't! I'm leaving now, too. I'm going to take a bus down there tonight."

"You can't do that." I said, not really knowing why she couldn't do it. It's not like he's in danger."

"He didn't raise his hand or anything. He's not sworn in." She started crying again. "If he's not sworn in, it's not too late to bring him back."

Didn't she know that it was irrelevant if he had sworn in or not? If he didn't get sworn into the army tonight, he was going to be swearing in front of a judge tomorrow. I felt annoyed that Alex would be so stupid in a crisis.

"Don't you have a shoot tomorrow?" I asked. "Maybe you should wait a few days."

There was silence on the other end. A big inhale, then, "I gotta run. There's a bus at midnight to Washington, then I can transfer to Columbia."

"Don't! Wait!" I yelled into the phone. "I'll be right over."

She clicked off and I slammed out of the loft, not bothering to close the door after myself. I ran the ten blocks to her apartment, tripping over cracks in the busted up sidewalks, once losing my bearings in the dark and going down the wrong street. By the time I got there, she was already gone. She hadn't locked her door either and I went into the kitchen, viewing the sad remains of their non-celebration. The unused cups and plates, the unopened bottles of wine. The real food, several trays of lasagna, were burning in the oven. I turned the oven off and ran out to the subway to get to Port Authority.

The individual bus portals of the bus station, row after row on either side of a long fluorescently lit corridor, all looked identical. I ran up to a bus driver who was collecting tickets to Harrisburg and asked him where I could get a bus to Washington. "Gate 83," he said, and as I ran down the corridor I finally saw her alone, sitting on a bench. Her nose was red and she clutched a little purse. She looked small and pathetic and I felt sorry for her, which was a new emotion. She reached in her purse and pulled out two tickets, handing one to me. She'd been expecting me, of course. In her eyes, the old rules still applied. We took our place at the end of the line and got on, sitting in the last available seats, in the back, next to the bathroom.

The ride was bumpy and neither of us slept. Alex spent a good part of the trip in the bathroom throwing up. "Motion sickness," she said, wiping her mouth on her sleeve, her sour breath almost making me sick. Neither of us had brought a toothbrush or a comb. Nothing. We arrived in Washington at three o'clock and Alex bought a powdered jelly donut at some dirty concession stand, where the sweets were set on top of yesterday's *Washington Posts*, before we joined another line of nocturnal commuters headed for Columbia, South Carolina. They were mostly long-haired boys, with the same destination as us: the reception station at Fort Jackson.

"Are you sure this thing isn't going to make you heave?" I took a bite of her donut, ravenous. "Don't you have to watch that?" I pointed to her stomach.

Alex said she didn't give a damn anymore. She wasn't going to model anymore, she was just going to follow Rick around. That was enough of a life for her. Following Rick. She stuffed the remainder of the stale pastry into her mouth.

"You mean, be a military wife?" I asked, incredulous. "Because that's what in store for you here. Unless he deserts, in which case you become the wife of a convict and you can visit him in prison."

"I love him," she said. "Why is that so hard to believe? People want to be with people they love."

We took our seats by the bathroom again, and it was a good thing, because Alex occupied it the whole time puking donut. I looked closely at her face. It had seemed fuller, which I'd attributed to tiredness and emotion, but now I understood and I panicked. My one avenue of escape was being blocked. Her jackknifed tractor-trailer was going to block the off-ramp. Alex was pregnant.

Chapter Nine

The sun was up and the air boiling by the time we arrived in Fort Jackson. A black drill sergeant greeted everyone who got off the bus, checking names off a roster. The boys stood in a loose configuration, their bell-bottom jeans and brightly colored shirts incongruous in the khaki colored camp. The drill sergeant bullied them to straighten up, tuck it in, tantalizing them with appointments he had made for them at the beauty parlor. One skinny boy, quite a wag on the bus, was on the ground doing pushups to—as the drill sergeant said—teach his tongue a lesson.

The drill sergeant approached us with evil glee, but became polite when he found out we weren't signed up for the army, that we just wanted to visit somebody.

"Reception over there, Ma'm," he said to Alex, touching the brim of his campaign hat. Nodding to me.

We walked over to the tin house that was the reception station. Rick's platoon was pulling supplies so we waited for him in the office, flipping through magazines. Lunch time came, and Rick's platoon was in the mess hall, so we went to a bar outside the post, The Outer Limits, to wait until four o'clock, when they said we could see him.

The most Alex could be pregnant was one month. "That's still enough time," I told her over a glass of Mad Dog 20/20 at the bar. "That's still early enough."

"I'm keeping it, Nadia," Alex said.

"What are you going to do with a baby?" I asked, trying to hide my desperation. "You can't take it with you on jobs. Anyway, it'll ruin your figure and you won't even get any jobs."

"I can't just...get *rid* of it." She shuddered.

100

"It's not even a baby yet," I said. "You won't be getting rid of anything. We're just starting out. A baby would end your life."

"I guess that's what my mother thought, too," she said. "I was ending her life."

I was stunned that Alex would have a thought that I wasn't privy to. We never talked about how lucky we were that her mother hadn't had an abortion. "That's the stupidest thing I ever heard of," I said, turning sharply from her, pretending that what she decided wouldn't affect me at all.

When we first came in, I'd noticed two Negro men in the corner booth, their eyes watery and unfocused by drink. Now one was beside me, his warm, whiskey breath crowding mine. He pulled out a ten dollar bill and waved it around until the bartender plunked down two more jelly glasses filled with MD 20/20 in front of us and two shots of whisky in front of him.

I raised my glass to him in thanks, waiting for him to crane his neck around to see Alex, but he held my gaze in his own dreamy brown one.

"I saw you watching me," he said.

"Did you?" I hadn't given him a thought before he appeared waving his money. He was wearing a polyester cream-colored shirt and white linen slacks; brown, Italian-cut shoes. His socks were sheer cream with ribs. He seemed unnaturally dressed up and well-groomed, like someone from a formal southern country. Most of the boys I knew, except for Lance who was so old he didn't count, belonged to the grungy jean and long hair race. I found him enticingly exotic. I swayed towards his warmth like a sapling seeking the sun through the forest ceiling.

"Jeremy," he said. Or maybe he said, "Jimmy." I couldn't understand him too well beneath his drawl.
The bartender lingered, wiping the counter raw in front of us, until I gave him a dirty look and he walked to the other end of the bar. Jeremy smiled and I felt myself go limp in a way I had previously

experienced only by reading novels. Jesus, no, I thought. Don't let me go all gooney on a colored boy.

At the pool table a few yards from the bar, balls were cracking as a young WAC hustled a couple of recruits. I turned on my barstool to get a look at the girl. She was petite, mocha-colored, with a cast on her right leg almost up to her hip. Her Afro was tipped in platinum, springing out from both ends of her barracks's cap. She chalked the stick and kept up a constant wave of trash talk to the two boys, pink and prickly as plucked chickens, who were pulling crumpled bills from their pockets and putting them on the edge of the pool table. When I caught her eye, she winked before bending over to methodically sink ball after ball and collect the pile of dough. The pink boys realized now they never had a chance, but were obliged to rack 'em up again.

"I couldn't help noticing how pretty you are," Jeremy said. "You're even prettier up close." He smiled, showing off his dazzling teeth and I waited for him to laugh, but he wasn't interested in the certified goddess on my right.

"I never claimed to be as smart as you," Alex said, oblivious to the conversation between Jeremy and me. "But I know what I want. I want a family."

"You have a family!" I said, reluctantly ripping my attention away from Jeremy. "What are you talking about? You have me!"

"I want my own family."

"Come on, Alex, be smart. In a few years you can have everything. A baby if you want. You've got to have a life first." I grabbed her wrist. "That's why we came to New York! To live. If we're smart we can have it all."

"Where did being smart ever get you? Work in a button store!"

"I'm an actress," I said, lifting my chin. I turned to smile at Jeremy in case he was listening, so he would realize that I wasn't just some white trash chick who hung around army bases picking up boys. I was an actress.

"That's right. I keep forgetting because you never act in anything. You know, Nadia, sometimes I think that you don't even see me for who I am. Just who you want me to be."

Jeremy wrote a number on a napkin and slipped it into my hand with a smile. His hand was so warm. Then he and his friend left. We had nothing else to do, so Alex and I drank up a fifth of Mad Dog, lurched off the barstools, and wandered back to post, tipsy. There was no sidewalk, and she seemed unnaturally unsteady, so I guided her by the elbow. The guard at the gate tried to give us a hard time about getting back in, but he only wanted to talk to Alex. I sighed. Even with no sleep, pregnant and vomit dribbling down her blouse, she was a man magnet.

By the time we got back to the reception area, Rick's platoon was off doing something else so we had to wait again.

"I'll marry him right here and now," Alex said, thinking that would solve something. "There's probably a chaplain around here somewhere. Jesus. What the hell is the delay." She got up and went to the counter. "What the hell is the delay?" she asked the private who was pecking steadily on an electric typewriter, as if that were his mission in life.

I stood on tiptoe and saw that he was copying a book, *On the Genealogy of Morals*. At the rate he was going, the project would last him the rest of his tour of duty. Of course, maybe that was the point.

He looked up at her and sniggered, checking out the clock on the wall. "Give the guy a break, lady. He just got here. Let him settle in, huh?"

She sat back down, disgruntled, rubbing her stomach, reassuring Little Rick inside that Big Rick would soon visit them, marry them, make them whole. I felt sick.

It wasn't until the clerk informed us that Rick's platoon was in the mess hall again, this time for dinner, that I finally got the idea that we wouldn't be seeing Rick tonight at all.

"Is that right?" I asked the clerk. I made a point of obviously checking out his nametag, Dougherty, as if I knew something spiteful to do with that knowledge. "We're not going to see him tonight, are we?"

Dougherty smiled and looked at the clock as if divining the future. "Why do you want to see him tonight? Give the guy a break, huh. It's bad enough being here, without having a couple of chicks hounding you. He's got to get his head into it, you know? Or he isn't going to survive."

Alex drew a sharp breath and put her hand to her throat dramatically. "Not survive?"

Dougherty grabbed a couple of keys from a pegboard. "You can bunk in the WAC shack. Tomorrow will be a little easier and you can sneak a peek at lover boy." He threw the keys across the counter and went in the back room, coming back with two piles of linens. "Across the company field." He pointed in the direction we were to go, put the linens in our hands and went back behind the counter, lit up a cigarette and held it between his lips as if he were blowing up a balloon and continued typing. Peck, peck, peck.

The WAC shack was a dormitory; twelve beds lined up against a wall, housing only one other occupant, the pool shark from the Outer Limits. She was reading. The leg in the cast stretched out across the bed, the undamaged one dangled off the side. She wore her fatigues and her Afro had a huge indentation, as if someone had mowed her hair where her hat had been.

She didn't look up when we came in, but I knew she saw us. I had seen her in action earlier that day, aware of every movement around her.

"Hello," I said, loudly. "Mind if we join you?"

She turned a page, making a big show of being in no hurry to acknowledge us.

I looked at the rows of beds. Bare mattresses on old springs. None looked inviting. "Are you saving these for anybody?"

"Anywhere you'd like." With that she flung her book on the bed, rising with some effort to inspect us. She swung her broken leg like Captain Ahab swinging his wooden peg around the deck.

Alex immediately flopped down on the bed next the WAC's. "God, it's hot in here. I don't think I've taken a normal breath in twelve hours. I don't believe I'll ever be able to breathe again."

Alex closed her eyes, knowing she was being admired. We watched her breathe for a while. The girl, whose name was, no lie, Marie Antoinette Bonaparte, was from Los Angeles via New Orleans. She had a master's degree in English Literature and was allergic to grass, which didn't make much difference when she was in Los Angeles, but was making her life hell in Fort Jackson. She had joined the army to escape the turmoil that was Los Angeles, hoping for a career in communications. The communications career she had in mind, perhaps a television or radio commentator, was different from the communications job the army actually needed her to do, which was to climb telephone poles and string wire between them. Actually, the army didn't need her, Marie Antoinette Bonaparte, specifically, to string wire. It was in fact, she admitted, a job she would never get to perform, because women weren't allowed in combat, the only possible scenario in which wire would need stringing without the benefit of a cherry picker. What the army really needed her to do was to go to the pole orchard every day, strap on her gaffs and shimmy to the top of a pole in order to shame men into doing the same.

"One boy was crying his eyes out, he was so scared to climb a puny telephone pole. When I got out there, he had to do it, or be a fag. He wasn't the only one, though. All the boys were scared. Men are pussies," Marie Antoinette said with authority.

I flinched at the word that I had never heard another woman use.

"If they sent us to Nam, we'd show them Cong pussies how to fight. They use their women. I've seen pictures of some of the dead soldiers, and they're women. Tits and everything. Women are vicious fighters, more vicious than men. They fight for keeps, to the death. Not for sport like men. Why do you think this thing is going on so long? We're not allowed to go in and just wipe them out. It's a game to those damned pussy generals."

She looked at me and all I could think of was "pussies" because she had said it so often, and I realized that was just the effect she wanted. She was a lesbian.

"Don't think I'm a man-hating lesbian," she said, reading my thoughts. "I like men as much as you do."

She gave me a sly smile, and I wondered if she could see something in me that I couldn't.

Alex got up suddenly. "Isn't there a fan or something in here? I'm going to die." She took off her blouse. "God this thing reeks." She flung it to the floor and went latrine.

"What a princess," Marie Antoinette said, but her eyes followed Alex.
I could tell she was already hooked. "She's my sister."

She didn't say anything about that. "You guys trying to get out?"
"Out?"
"Of the service."
"We're not in."
"Want to go shoot some pool?"
"I saw you this afternoon."
"Was that you?" She sat down on the bed, the flop causing the bed to move a couple of inches on the highly polished floor. Involuntarily, she tried to stop the skid with her cast and winced. "Damn."

We made Alex put on her soiled blouse and dragged her to the Outer Limits, despite protests that if she couldn't see Rick, she'd rather curl up in a ball and die. Marie Antoinette marked a couple of recruits at the bar. She nudged me and showed me with her eyes that she had them in her sights. We took stools next to them, and within minutes the boys were explaining to a prettily befuddled Alex what the chalk was, what the stick was for and some laws of physics that ruled the world of spinning balls and their impact on each another.

"They're so stupid I almost hate to do this." Marie Antoinette hobbled over to the boys and suggested that playing for money would make things more interesting, and within minutes she had appropriated all the money they planned to use to go home with the next weekend.

Alex and I looked down into our drinks, cherry colored wine of the cough syrup variety and swirled them as if they were cocktails at the Ritz in New York.

"She's nice," Alex said.

"Who?"

"Marie Antoinette."

"Oh." I was surprised that Alex even remembered her name. "Well, she certainly likes you."

"What do you mean, 'like?'" Alex asked.

"You like girls now?" I asked, snorting my derision.

"No! I was just asking what you meant by 'like.' I mean, I like her too."

"Not like that!"

"Did you ever think to try it?" Alex asked. She eyed the other patrons.

"No!" I rotated the glass madly.

Alex smiled and I wanted to choke it out of her. She had gone down avenues I hadn't even considered and she wasn't going to tell me unless I begged. Which I refused to do. I suddenly yearned to be rid of her, and I caught my breath at the thought. I could just run from this place, take the first bus back home. Wherever that was. And that was what stopped me. My home had always been Alex. Who was it now? Lance? Was home, for me, always going to be other people, the most unreliable real estate on earth?

A moan came from the boys at the pool table as they realized that Marie Antoinette had fleeced them. A low murmur as they negotiated the next game, trying to win back what they had lost. They were betting money they hadn't even earned yet. They wouldn't have enough for a beer for months if they kept playing. But the balls cracked, fell, and soon our Marie was sitting on the stool next to Alex, grinning, treating us to more vile refreshment.

"It was almost a shame to do it to them," she said. "This is what boredom will do to you." The boys were two months in hock to her.

"You should have left them something. Money, dignity," I said.

"Like hell. When you have the enemy on the ropes, you got to finish him off or he'll rise up later and kill you."

"Is that something you learned in the army?" I asked.

"Los Angeles."

We walked slowly back to the barracks, aware of and trying to ignore, Marie Antoinette's limp. The air was stifling and I undressed self-consciously in front of Marie, who whipped off her clothing without thinking. I thought of the strip tease I had done for the store detective in Macy's, the poses for Mr. Thwaite, and even the session with Star, the artist. I had been blissfully aware that my body, however imperfect, was more than adequate to them. But when in close proximity to Alex, whose body was a work of breathtaking perfection, I felt defeated.

Marie Antoinette watched Alex undress and I could see her fingers trembling, wishing they were on that body, as she put her crutches in her wall locker and hopped back onto her bed. Alex, nude and beautiful, lay on top of the sheets, it was so hot there was an excuse other than the sheer exhibitionism. She was asleep almost immediately. I sat next to Marie Antoinette her on bed.

"My sister's name is Jean D'Arc," she said as if I had asked about her family. "She's even more beautiful than her." We looked at the slumbering body that was impossible, really, to ignore. "Black girls are more beautiful than white girls. There's nothing pretty about all those blue veins showing through skin. And those skinny lips. They're like chickens."

"I never said there was," I said, as if I had to defend white womanhood. I hadn't realized there was a competition.

"It's more competitive than you think," she said, once again reading my mind.

"What's more competitive?"

"Jean D'Arc had more lovers than anybody I've ever known, male or female. It was as if she wanted everyone to enjoy her beauty. It was like this treasure that had been dropped in the middle of everything, and she wanted to share. It was very cool, really. She was so non-possessive with it."

"How many lovers have you had?" I asked.

"I never counted."

I didn't believe her, knowing that if I rifled her belongings I would find something with notches carved in it.

"You've had two," she said, "And they've both been disappointing."

"Why did you join the Army?"

"To get away from Jean D'Arc."

"I thought you loved her."

She sighed loudly. "Love. Sure I loved her. I just couldn't be an introduction to her forever. At some point, you want someone to say, you know, you're not so bad yourself. People are fucking lemmings in love."

We swung our feet off the side of the bed, said goodnight. I waited to hear soft breathing coming from my bunkmates then I pulled my jeans on and slid soundlessly out the door, nervously fraying the napkin with Jeremy's number on it, looking for a phone booth in the moonlit Carolina night. Finally, I saw one outside the orderly room. I dropped a nickel in the slot and dialed his number, feeling how warm I imagined his skin to be when the phone picked up and a woman's shrill voice answered.

"Who's there?" she demanded. I had expected Jeremy's molasses voice and was struck dumb, literally, by the feminine voice. There was a party going on in the background. Jazzy music and female laughter. "What do you want?"

I slipped the phone back into its cradle and walked back towards the barracks, thinking of Jeremy and the party I was missing. Was that his woman who answered the phone? A man like Jeremy would have several women, but only one that he let answer his telephone.

"What do you want?" that woman had asked.

I strolled outside the gates and climbed up a hill outside the post and sat down beneath a row of pines, enjoying, if not exactly a breeze, at least the freshness of the green trees. The needles were like a mattress.

I thought of the women who would be at that party, dark and sultry women wearing too-tight satin dresses that showed off curves that would be considered vulgar by white standards. Jeremy was dancing with the woman who answered the phone. She was wearing a red dress that dipped around her breasts and draped her hips in a suggestive way. I pictured that she didn't shave under her arms and the sight of that hair drove Jeremy into a frenzy of desire for her. She wasn't very pretty, I knew. Jeremy would never like a pretty woman, because a pretty woman had too many options and Jeremy wanted to keep all the options for himself. The thought that Jeremy had the options would keep that woman in the red dress hanging around, hungering for him. "What do you want?" she had asked me.
I lay down under the tree and put my hand between my legs, moving it until I came and felt sleepy. Under the trees was peaceful and as good a place to sleep as any. I said aloud to Jeremy's woman, as if she were still on the phone, talking to me, waiting for me to reply. "I want the same thing as you."

Chapter Ten

I woke just after dawn. The sun was already so hot under the trees that sweat rolling into my eyes tickled me awake and I wandered back down to the post, brushing the pine needles off my backside. The guard, same boy as yesterday, didn't say anything, as if he was used to women coming in looking as if they had slept in the woods. He gave me a half-assed salute.

I wasn't really surprised to see a particular dark-skinned lemming in bed with my sister. Outside, platoons of recruits sang in a call and response cadence as they ran through the early morning, getting their exercise before the sun burned all the ambition out of them.

"Jody was there when you left."
"You're right!"
"Bubba was there when you left."
"You're right!"
"Sound off!"
"One, two."
"Sound off!"
"Three, four."
"One, two, three, four. One, two….three, four!"

The song had lines about how Bubba stole your girlfriend, your Cadillac, your job, *your life* while you were busy doing this silly-assed Army stuff. One drill sergeant sang the cadence while another one brought up the rear of the formation, taunting by name the soldiers who were having a hard time keeping up.

The singing woke Alex and Marie Antoinette, and they moaned as they let themselves be dragged awake. I met my sister's eyes and she let me know, without saying a word, that what had happened was none of my damned business. When Alex went into the bathroom to shower, I hurriedly slipped off my jeans and sandals.

"You can borrow my stuff. Soap and shampoo," Marie Antoinette said. "Alex is using them now. But when she's finished."

When she's finished, I get her crumbs.

Marie examined her fingernails as if her fortune were revealed there.

"What happened to Jean D'Arc," I asked, snapping her out of her happy reveries.

"Pregnant. She got pregnant and couldn't figure out who the father was. Not that that was a big deal." She glared at me lest I think less of Jean D'Arc for sleeping around. "But being pregnant was. It sort of made her features all go down to the ground, like they had run out of energy. And her hair lost its luster. It just wasn't the same. I read once that the only difference between great beauties and normal people is a matter of centimeters. A few centimeters one way or the other is what makes some people mesmerizing and the rest of us forgettable." She made a swirling motion, making sure to include us both among the damned.

"Well, being pregnant couldn't have altered that," I said, "those centimeters. She must still have that."

"She just looks tired. She is tired. Always running after Darlin. Her baby."

We looked up at the same time to see Alex standing naked in the aisle holding a towel in one hand as if she didn't know what to do with it, didn't want to just drop it on the ground, her other hand cupping her tummy, where her own Darlin was lurking, waiting to rob Alex of her beauty, her youth, her future, because Darlin *was* the future and once she was born it would no longer belong to Alex. The idea that people are mere receptacles for the next generation is perhaps the cruelest knowledge that youth can have. That you count for nothing except as a propagator of the species. Who wants to know that the universe regards you as a Matryoshka doll holding a smaller, and slightly dissimilar for genetic purposes, version of yourself? The answer is no one. Our egos are way too big to take in both our desires of the moment as well as a picture of the grand plan. Unfortunately, the light doesn't illuminate that particular map until a little bugger is tugging at your intestines and pulling stretch marks down your hips, like ropes from which he will swing from tree to tree, yelping his victory cry of life.

We dressed in silence. Marie Antoinette had to report to the Commanding Officer before she was free to waste the day in the Outer Limits. The Army at least had to *know* where she was. Marie Antoinette had quite a racket going, all for the pain of a broken leg. She slipped a wad of bills into my hand, "in case we don't meet up later," she said. I waited until she was done looking back at Alex, waving good-bye, then finally out of sight in the Headquarters' Building, before I relaxed my fist and counted the money. Forty dollars. It would get us home and then some. I breathed as if I had been holding my breath for days. I tried not to prorate Alex's prostitution. But I couldn't help it. Five dollars an hour. That was the price of knowing Alex in the biblical sense.

Dougherty didn't say anything when we appeared once again in his orderly room. He was right where we left him, fingering the letters of *On the Geneology of Morals*, like he was carving the Rosetta Stone. His blond hair, while longer than allowed the recruits, was greasy and matted in a swirling pattern around his head, as if a helicopter had landed on it. His uniform was so wrinkled it was obvious he had slept in it with no more respect than the draft resisters who wore the green as satire. I wondered if he was aware of the words he was typing, or if, after a hundred pages he would notice the page and say, "Oh, my God! What is this crap?"

He looked up when he felt my stare. "He's been waiting for an hour in the day room."

"Which would be where?" I was annoyed that we had wasted so much time and no one had notified us.

Dougherty pointed to the door of a hallway while going back to his typing. "End of the hall, two flights down."

We followed the sound of smacking pool balls. The Army was starting to seem like a subversive organization that was secretly schooling the nation's next generation of pool sharks.

Alex, during all this, was quiet. She no longer seemed anxious to see Rick, more resigned. She glided into the room pausing in the doorway, as good-looking people do, to give everyone a chance to get used to the fact that the locus of attention has shifted.

"Jesus!" A young man with dark stubble over his misshapen head smiled through his discolored and crooked teeth at us. His narrow face looked familiar. It took a minute to register that it was Rick.

"Jesus, yourself," I said, so glad he looked terrible I almost laughed aloud. I couldn't help thinking that this is what Samson in the Bible must have looked like when he was shorn. In a weird way, it was cosmic symmetry. I did laugh.

"It's short, I know," he grinned and ran his fingers, bony and yellow, over the moon-like landscape of his head. He tried to get Alex's attention, but she stared stonily away. "Baby, what are we going to do?" It was impossible that he was unaware of how ridiculous he looked, but there it was. He was blissed-out thinking that his rock n'roll persona could somehow translate into army drab; impervious to the fact that the thing Alex loved about him was anything other than the illusion he spun with his guitar and long hair. Without those things, he was just another cull in a barnyard full of them.

"How's the little one?" he whispered, sidling up to her and touching her .

"Stop it!" she slapped his hand away.

"Hey!" He looked hurt. "What's the matter? Aren't you glad to see me?"

"Of course, I'm glad to see you. I'm here aren't I? It was just a long trip down here and I'm exhausted." She seemed confused by her own revulsion.

"I know, little mother."

"I'm not your little mother," she said.

"Hey, I'm the father, aren't I?"

"Of course, you're the father. When do I ever get a minute away from you? Jesus, no one would even have a minute to slip it in."

"Is that a complaint, or what? You want some time alone for someone else to slip it in?" He frowned, which was no more becoming on his awkward features than a smile.

"I had a bad night." She looked down at the floor as if she had tossed and tumbled all night because of the wretched humidity, rather than in the arms of a lesbian with a broken leg. "Sorry. It just seems so hopeless. I don't know...I don't know what I was thinking."

Recently, the evidence had been piling up (to me, at least) that to become an adult meant a paring down of illusions until you reach the core truth, which is this: any perceived advantage you start out with is equalized somewhere down the line. Beauty fades. Fortunes are spent. Brains can get twisted. Even good intentions can be strangled in the bitter tangle of unfulfilled desires.

"So are we going or what?" Rick whispered, looking around surreptitiously, thinking that someone cared what he was saying.

"Aren't you kind of like, stuck here now? I mean, you're sworn in and everything."

I could tell she was trying not to, but she couldn't help but stare at the rugged terrain that was the top of Rick's head. I couldn't either. It was truly a marvel that something assumed to be more or less *round* could have so many gullies and straggly clumps. I forced myself to concentrate instead on the incredible shine that seemed to be on everyone's combat boots.

Rick pushed Alex into a corner and whispered something urgently in her ear, and she brushed him off. He grabbed her arm.

"I said okay. Okay!" she said, turning abruptly, leaving Rick smoothing his ugly head, glaring. "Let's get out of here," se said, brushing by me. I followed mutely, shrugging at Rick. "I don't know why I came here."

We blew past Dougherty in the orderly room. He looked up from his self-imposed penance to say, "See gorgeous George?" and as an act of kindness said, "Next bus to D.C. leaves at half-past. Right outside the gate."

We went outside to wait in the dusty road. Clumps of Carolina pines were everywhere, but they did nothing to relieve the heat that undulated around us. I could tell by the sun's high position that it was close to eleven-thirty.

"I don't need him to have my baby," she said, tugging her blouse tightly around her middle. "I don't need anyone."

"You don't need him," I agreed.

We sat on a guardrail that was still a little tacky from being recently painted and I had to look to make sure no paint was getting on my jeans. The guard at the gate came out of his little hut to stare at Alex, but eventually he got bored with that and went back in to review the girlie magazine that a thousand guards before him had read. He tossed that aside when he saw the bus coming down the road from the pines, and came out to inform us of that fact as if we couldn't see.

"There's the bus," he shouted.

I waved. "Thanks."

Alex tapped her foot trying to accelerate the bus's arrival.

"He sure got ugly looking," I volunteered, saying what was on both of our minds.

Alex's chest heaved. "You slept with him too. He was good enough for you." She walked a little down the road, as if meeting the bus would hurry our departure from this sandy hell-hole.

And then we saw him, Rick running down the path that led from his barracks to the gate. He was carrying a backpack and all I could think was that he looked like a little boy running away from home.

The guard saw him and picked up his rifle, just as the bus pulled up in front of us.

"Jesus," Alex said, as detached as if she was watching a television show, "what the hell does he think he's doing?"

She boarded the bus with a regal glance at the driver, leaving me to fish around for the money Marie Antionette had shoved in my hand. The driver, a black man with big sad eyes that made me think of Jeremy, nodded politely and checked his passengers in the rear-view mirror. You could tell he didn't give a damn what anybody did, he just didn't want any trouble. The bus was half-filled with freaks. We sat in the middle. It was an old bus with windows that pushed up and no bathroom, and Alex took the seat by the window so I didn't see right away that the guard had Rick in his rifle's sight. It was only after I sensed that the attention in the bus had shifted to the scene outside that I saw Rick, frozen between the guard and the bus.

They both looked scared: two boys stuck in roles in someone else's play. Neither wanted to be where he found himself then, certainly not in an Army uniform. Their positions could have been switched, and it wouldn't have made a difference. The guard was stuck in an unnatural position, his rifle on his shoulder, squinting at Rick, at the bus, at the bus driver who didn't want any trouble, but who seemed about to receive a bucketful. Rick was immobile, frozen in the act of running, one arm propelling him up, one leg stretched out, his little knapsack still swinging from his hand. Everyone in the bus watched as Rick and the guard faced off.

The guard shouted something and Rick answered. I couldn't make out what they were saying. Rick turned slowly, keeping his hands in the air. They talked some more and I let out a breath as the guard lowered his rifle and looked at the bus. Suddenly, the guard relaxed, resting the butt of his rifle on his toe and Rick scrambled aboard, moving down the aisle. He plopped in the seat in front of us, twisting to kneel on it and looked back happily, his misshapen head looming over us like the cratered moon. The driver closed the door and quickly drove away.

"Hey," Rick said to Alex, but she crossed her arms and looked out the window.

I shrugged.

A blond girl wearing an Indian skirt and a red dot painted between her blue-eyes leaned across the aisle and put a nail-bitten hand on Rick's leg. She held out a joint. "Here, man. That was so heavy. I couldn't believe what that pig was going to do."
Rick took a long drag . He checked out the girl while he held his breath and passed the joint to me. He held the smoke in and choked a little, but still he smiled at the girl. Everyone around us turned to give approving looks to Rick. He was some kind of hero for having not been shot.

"What did that pig say to you?" the girl asked.

"Good luck," Rick said. "He said, 'good luck'."

He pulled his wallet from his hip pocket and flipped through some cards, finally finding a dog-eared photo of himself with his band, and held it out for the girl to examine. "That's really me," he said.

You're a musician!" the girl said. "Cool. My old man is a musician, too."

Rick looked around to see if her old man was with her and was going to beat the shit out of him for poaching on his territory, but no one seemed interested in their mutual attraction except me.

"Don't worry, man, he's cool. He's in California." The girl laid her hand on Rick's leg and they both seemed content with that arrangement. Rick was turned completely around and apparently forgot the reason, Alex and their baby, that he had jumped ship in the first place.

I stared out the window trying to remember that I was happy just last week when Lance and I went to Woodstock. I wanted to dwell on that happiness for a while to erase the increasing misery that was crowding this bus. But remembering it no longer pleased me. It was like looking at someone else's photo album and feeling bored. In misery, then, I rode in silence. A patch of pines was the only thing to occasionally break the spell until we pulled into the outskirts of Charlotte for a rest stop, the bus driver told us, where there was nothing but a Dairy Queen, a bathroom, and two military police who were sitting in their Jeep and smoking until Rick descended from the bus. They casually extinguished the butts on the side of their vehicle, stripped them down to the filter, which they shoved in their pockets before swinging their legs onto the ground, holding their rifles in a noticeably firmer grip than the guard at Fort Jackson. Alex wanted to wait until the others had come back so she wouldn't have to stand in line for the Lady's Room, so she didn't see the MP poke a finger into Rick's chest then nudge him to the back seat of the Jeep where they strapped him in with some kind of locked seatbelt and handcuffed him. The blond girl was already in the bathroom, so it was only me on deck waving his ship good-bye.

"Take care!" I yelled, and I remember that Rick searched the small crowd for the source of that cry and seeing only me, hung his poor gnarly head. Some of the people from the bus, pulled from their own world by Rick's drama, began shouting at the MPs. The Jeep ground gears and made dust tracking out of the Dairy Queen parking lot, while the crowd chanted "Death to the Pigs" and Rick held his manacled hands over his head in a feeble peace sign.

Chapter Eleven

We found out later that Rick was court-marshaled and sent to Ft. Leavenworth. A few letters arrived from him, asking about the baby. I opened them when it became apparent that Alex wasn't going to. I was curious what turns his life would take after being led off in handcuffs by two MPs outside a dusty little town in North Carolina. He told us about his court marshal, which he called a kangaroo court. He called the presiding officers Nazis. His own military defense lawyer went through the motions of defending him, he said, but he could tell it was just an AWOL gig to the guy, who wanted the trial to be over so he could start the serious drinking that defined his life.

"Juiceheads," Rick wrote, in a philosophical manner new to him, "are such pricks."

He wrote of the tedium of his cell, but kept insisting he would get out shortly. He said that his father was some big shot in Coca-Cola and had hired a civilian lawyer to try get his delinquent son's ass out of the can and keep the family name out of the paper.

I didn't want to answer questions about the baby, so I didn't write back. Mostly because there was no more baby to talk about. When we disembarked at Port Authority, we headed to Lance's loft. Lance. He was the closest thing to home we both had, and it didn't occur to us that we wouldn't be wanted. And Lance came through, welcoming Alex home, albeit with a lack of mania that made it clear that during our absence he'd gotten over her. He bought a second-hand box-spring and mattress so Alex could sleep alone, bought new sheets with little yellow flowers all over them to cheer her, and was genuinely solicitous in the way a brother would be for his sister. I wondered then at the fickleness of love, but really, what he loved about Alex was the same thing that I did. She was a blank screen on which we projected our fantasies.

His lack of ardor infuriated Alex, and she turned on me, insisting that she still wanted to have the baby and that all I did was make her crazy with reasons to get rid of it. Dr. Lombardi turned up on our third day back and she immediately began interrogating him, saying she just wanted to know her alternatives. He told her she had two. The first was that if you were less than eight weeks pregnant you could take a combination of two pills that together would block the hormones needed to maintain a pregnancy. He ticked off the side effects, and this was if they worked and they sometimes didn't: cramping, diarrhea, vomiting. By the time he got to heavy bleeding Alex was in tears and so was I. He pulled a brown vial from his pocket and tapped two black and green Libriums into her palm and one into mine.

Her other choice was to have an abortion. "I know someone in Jersey City," he said. "They're good. Medical people, not back alley people."

Abortions were illegal. Underground legend was full of girls who descended into back alley abortion clinics and never came back or returned twisted beyond recognition.

"First trimester, there shouldn't be complications," Dr. Lombardi said, "But the sooner the better."

After a half hour of declaiming she wasn't sure what she wanted, wasn't sure whether to go through with it, most of the time spent glaring at me as if the whole screwed up situation was my fault, which I was beginning to believe, Alex finally told Dr. Lombardi to make the arrangements.

"I'll do it from a pay phone," he said and left.

I called our brother John through the gallery where his paintings had sold and told him what had happened. I told Alex that the more people who knew what was going on, the better, but really I was scared. More scared than I had been in my entire life and I wanted a trustworthy adult involved.

Dr. Lombardi was chain-smoking when he came to apartment the following morning to tell us where to go. "Do you have the money?" he asked Alex who shut her eyes and held up an envelope stuffed with five hundred dollars, money that she saved up from her modeling gigs.

"Does anyone have any weed?" Alex asked. "I could use a toke."

Dr. Lombardi pulled a joint from his shirt pocket and flipped it to Lance. "Fire it up, but only a little. They're going to need to know if she's feeling any pain."

John had arrived with coffee and donuts an hour earlier and was squashed in a beanbag chair in the corner, clenching and unclenching his hands. He waved away the joint when it came to him.

"These things aren't that bad," I said, not having a clue what I was talking about. "Girls do it all the time."

"Maybe if we had a real doctor," John hissed.

Dr. Lombardi shot him a dirty look. The phone rang. It was like a telephone ringing in church while the priest was saying mass. A model wannabe on the other end, oblivious to our little drama, wanted to schedule some time for a shoot. Lance checked his watch, then looked back at us, trying to figure out how long our business was going to take and mumbled something into the receiver before hanging up. He went to the window and put both hands on it, stretching himself like a cat, then picked up his wallet from the kitchen table, gave me a thumbs-up sign and walked out. And that was that.

Alex, John and I took the subway from St. Marks Place to Penn Station and then walked underground to the Path train that ran under the Hudson River to Jersey City. As instructed we got off at the third stop, Journal Square, climbed the steps, crossed Kennedy Boulevard, a four-lane two ways street, and stood on the curb outside the Loew's

Jersey Theater, a slightly run-down colossal 1920s movie palace showing *Midnight Cowboy*. It was seven o'clock when we emerged from the subway. We were to wait there until the line of people for the eight o'clock show had gone in then cross back over Kennedy Boulevard and stand in front of the subway steps. A car would come for Alex. They'd be watching and know by what we did who were were.

"Only one of us is supposed to be here," I told John.

"They'll be here," John said. "Why don't you get a soda and I'll wait with Alex." There was a soda shop at the corner. We both sat back on the curb next to Alex instead.

Forty-five minutes passed. The mercury vapor streetlights snapped on, making us look like ghouls. Alex started to cry. "Maybe they aren't coming," she said. A half hour passed.

"Let's get out of here," John said, and we all stood up, jumped up in relief really, when a black Buick four-door with tinted windows pulled up to the curb.

The passenger side window opened a crack and an unnaturally high voice asked, "Which one of you is it?" Alex raised her hand like a little girl in kindergarten class. "Did you bring your payment," and Alex held up her envelope like an admission ticket to an amusement park ride. "Get in!" high voice commanded and when the back door opened I saw another girl in the back seat.

"Hey," John said, "What do we do?"

"Wait. We'll drop her off later," high voice said. The window rolled up and the car pulled away and I had the scary thought that we would never see Alex again.

Later, Alex told us that the procedure itself didn't take so long, but they had to drive around, picking up four other girls first. They let them out at the service entrance of an apartment building, rode the service elevator to the fifth floor, and went through a kitchen into a large apartment that had been turned into a kind of hospital emergency room: florescent lights, gurneys, heavily curtained windows, two doctors and two nurses. They lined the six of them up in adjoining hospital beds separated by curtains, did the procedure, gave them Tylenol and a sanitary napkin, then loaded them back in the car dropping them off in the reverse order they picked them up. It was way past midnight when the Buick pulled up and Alex got out, looking wiped out.

"We should have never let her go through with it," John said. "I would have raised it."

"Leave it alone," I commanded. We had spent the almost four hours we were waiting drinking beer John had brought in brown paper bags and arguing about what ifs and I was sick of it.

"No one talked to me the whole time," Alex said, as if the impersonality of the way she'd been treated was what had impressed her the most. John put his arm around her and pulled her down the subway stairs and we went home to a loft where Dr. Lombardi was alone, watching television.

Alex ignored Dr. Lombardi who said, "How ya holding up, sister?" and she immediately conked out on her new mattress in the corner. The contents of her purse had spilled out when she threw it on the kitchen counter and when I gathered up the stuff from the floor to shove back in her bag I picked up a yellow packet that looked like a dial with Ortho Novo embossed on the top. Pills were encased in a plastic ring around the inside of the dials. The Pill. The people at the abortion clinic must have given them to her. I found a bottle of bourbon that Lance had been hoarding. The Guru appeared with a joint and a deck of cards, ("Life," he said, "must go on!") and it seemed as if we were going to have a poker game but John wouldn't play and we all got sad from the dope and the booze and stared glumly at the baby ghost floating around the room.

"At a regular wake, we would have stories to tell about the deceased," John said. His voice, subdued, belied the turmoil in his face.

"John, there is no wake," I said, "There is no person."

He leaned forward and grabbed my hand, holding it hard. "She was your niece."

I began to panic as I realized I was letting a temporarily deranged person define how to view this thing. This it.

Alex shot up. "For God's sake, John. She was nothing. A little nothing. And I want us to stop talking about the damned thing right now." She turned her back to us and the floating baby ghost.

I felt an indefinable ache that I tried to beat out of myself by banging my head against the doorjamb but it did nothing to relieve the feeling of helplessness. Hopelessness. I have felt that same thing in later years when people I loved have left me or didn't want me in the first place. But the first time, as they say, is best and that night the pain in my soul was so excruciating, it almost crossed the line into pleasure. But of course, I had a history of turning pain into pleasure.

Dr. Lombardi, the only one of us who was vaguely knowledgeable about death had ingested one of his pocket comestibles and was lying on my futon, staring up at the ceiling. The Guru was shuffling and re-shuffling his deck of cards. John and I held hands, and when Lance came in, noisy and wondering that our little wake was still in session, for the first time I felt real joy on seeing him.

"What do we do?" I was on my feet ready to follow instructions from anybody who would tell me that if I did or thought one particular thing, everything would be all right.

"You girls certainly botched this thing, didn't you?" he said. He saw his bottle of bourbon on the floor and confiscated it. "Two idiots pretending to be grown-ups."

"Just one thing I ask," he said, pointing an index finger at my brother then a thumb at the door. "Got it? It's not a hotel."

John, by this time, had started sobbing. I put a hand on his shoulder then pulled him to the door. He and the Guru followed me down the stairwell and, reluctant to be alone, we sat on the steps and smoked cigarettes and talked about our families until the sun finally came up. And that, as they say, was that.

I tried to pretend that everything was normal after that, but everything seemed to have shifted two steps back. I couldn't find the nerve to go back to the button store. I didn't even call Shel to tell him what had happened to me and he probably thought I had died. After his kindness, I owed him more than that, but it wasn't until much later that I realized how thoughtless I had been to leave him wondering and worrying. He probably took on another project. There are people who seem helplessly attracted to projects, and, this is not a value judgment on Shel or his kind, it is just recognition that I am not one of them. That's what I learned that summer: what I am capable and incapable of, how much I am different from my fellow humans, but mostly how much I am like everyone else. We aren't unique like snowflakes, as they tell you when you are a child. Yeah, everyone is slightly different, though the variations aren't enough to find solace in. But neither are they enough to make you despair. Anyway, I never again allowed myself to pass Shel's Button Emporium because what would I say to Shel? Better that he think the worst of me and know that nothing he had to give would have freed me from my own rotten self. And there have been others in my life, other places where the parting was so unsatisfying that I never again allowed myself to walk down that street, and soon I found myself, like everyone else, living in a narrowing section of the world. The only difference between me and others is the names of the streets.

Alex recovered after a brief convalescence, in which Lance and I, despite our swearing that we loved her no longer, competed for her favor. She did go back to work, but the jobs were fewer and paid less well than before. She had dried up a little, which seems like a funny thing to say of an eighteen year old girl, but it's true. Her little baby took a little of Alex with her into the Jersey City sewer system. Mother Nature has seen many great beauties of all species bloom, and an equal number of great beauties fade in a ruthless inevitable procession.

I did try out for a play. I danced nude in front of a handful of people, all wearing business suits and peering out at me from the dark audience and I felt….nothing. I wasn't exhilarated; I wasn't anything, really. My nudity had lost its power to shame or excite me. I put on the mask I had learned to create as a little girl, recreating the scenes of my own life that I saw in my father's film, and I knew I was doing a credible job. But the thrill was gone.

"I see the fire in your heart," the casting director told me as he wrestled me out of my clothes in his office after the audition. He was a blubbery man who smelled of liquor and what I later found out was Fixodent. I had never kissed a set of dentures before and I couldn't stop thinking of George Washington. I told him it wasn't him, that I was very confused sexually, that sex had never been as much fun in reality as it was in my fantasies, which I then found out was the most provocative thing a woman could tell a man and I barely escaped with my bottom still attached.

He was, however, willing to forgive my frigidity. He thought I could act. He thought I could dance and he wanted me in his play. "This is going to rock Broadway. Then London. This is your way into the world. Believe me, Nadia, once the world sees you naked, they won't stop thinking about you."

There it was. The thing I had been waiting to hear all summer. But it was too late to cheer me, and when he suggested we try a position from the Kamasutra to get at that damned frigidity, I told him I had changed my mind. I didn't want to act anymore. I was going back to school.

Chapter Twelve

Most everyone recovers from youth, and I suppose I did too. My overwhelming concern of "who am I?" and "how am I special" metamorphosed into the duller, but more compelling issue of, what am I going to *now*? I applied for admission to Columbia and, perhaps because the nobler minds of my generation were concerned with issues much larger than themselves and were pursuing goals outside of the ivory tower, there was a space for me and I had only to await the spring term to be admitted and some semblance of real life to begin.

Instead of hanging around the loft with an indifferent Lance and a cold Alex, I spent most of my days in the public library reading room, where I was surprised to see the Guru, hunched in a corner, a stack of books in front of him, coolly completing *New York Times Sunday* crossword puzzles. He looked up once to wet the tip of his pencil with his tongue and nodded at me politely as he would at any stranger, and continued to fill in the answers to the puzzles as fast as he could read the clues. I took the seat next to him and we enjoyed a comfortable sort of chumminess, he solving puzzles and me trying to absorb as much information about anything as I could to make up for my recent mental sloth until the spring semester began. That day in September when I left the library, we smiled companionably. And then I never saw him again.

Alex left one October morning before she thought anyone was awake. Although I heard her, I made no move to stop her and let her get on with her leaving. She took no more than she came with: a Samsonite cosmetics case and some bottles of shampoo. Even though some of them were mine, I didn't begrudge her. She was never greedy about material goods. Lance must have heard her too, because he wasn't surprised to see her gone. He did ask, however, when did I think I would be moving out?

Alex got a job on a television soap opera, *Through a Glass Darkly*. A newfound world-weary look combined with her mesmerizing features proved irresistible to the camera. So she stole that dream of mine, too.

I graduated honorably from Columbia, then went to law school on a scholarship that my brother helped me to dredge up and became a New York public defender, defending such human wreckage as Ethiopian heroin smugglers who for a thousand dollars stuff condoms full of junk worth a hundred times that and swallow them to get past customs. Or poor deranged souls who shove human beings in front of subway cars. My acting ability comes in handy here as I convince myself and then juries that scum is worth defending. Sometimes, when the prosecution is sloppy, I win a case. But they are always guilty, and always I ask the question: What was the name of that road that they decided to go down and how did they get so lost?

I said that everyone survives youth, but that's not exactly true. Our brother, John, and I fought like crazy after Alex's abortion. John blamed himself for not stopping Alex, even though I tried to tell him there was no stopping her. Then he blamed both himself and me for being complicit in "murder" he said. Like any two people who know and love each other anyway, we knew precisely where our arrows would do the most harm and so we had some near fatal hits before we just stopped seeing each other. A few years later, I ran into his lover Glenn on Hudson Street, and Glenn said I should really stop by and see John, who was dying of a disease that didn't yet have a name. John let me hold one of his hands while our father, whom he kept in touch with over the years, came out of nowhere to hold his other hand. Our father, overcome with the emotion of his son's death, or perhaps just to readjust the count of his legitimate children, told me then that Alex was his biological daughter. Mrs. Pembroke, the woman he eventually left my mother for, had their child and deposited it in our garbage can, because she just couldn't cope. She thought she was just giving back to him what was his.

I never told Alex, mostly because I never see her in any but the most non-intimate settings. And I want her to be happy. How would it make it her feel to know that her own father and her real mother, her own family, lived on our block the whole time? That her one ace didn't win her the most basic game of all, a parents' love? I can't tell her because I want her to be happy. She's my sister and I love her. I want her to be happy. I love her. I really do.

.

e.

ABOUT THE AUTHOR

Maddy Wells is the pen name of Bathsheba Monk.
www.bathshebamonk.com

www.ingramcontent.com/pod-product-compliance
Lightning Source LLC
Chambersburg PA
CBHW020916180626
46816CB00007BA/2425

* 9 7 8 0 9 9 9 1 4 6 0 5 7 *